T0322293

The Everyman Wodehouse

P. G. WODEHOUSE

The Pothunters

EVERYMAN

Published by Everyman's Library
50 Albemarle Street
London W1S 4BD

First published by A. & C. Black Ltd., 1902
Published by Everyman's Library, 2009

Copyright by The Trustees of the Wodehouse Estate
All rights reserved

Originally appeared in *Public School Magazine*, January, February, March 1902 with illustrations by R. Noel Pocock. For the book the frontispiece and nine full page illustrations were taken from the magazine serial.

Typography by Peter B. Willberg

ISBN 978-1-84159-167-4

A CIP catalogue record for this book is available from the British Library

Distributed by Penguin Random House UK,
20 Vauxhall Bridge Road, London SW1V 2SA

Typeset by AccComputing, North Barrow, Somerset
Printed and bound in Germany
by CPI books GmbH, Leck

The Pothunters

TO

JOAN, EFFIE AND
ERNESTINE BOWES-LYON

CONTENTS

1 PATIENT PERSEVERANCE PRODUCES PUGILISTIC PRODIGIES

'Where *have* I seen that face before?' said a voice. Tony Graham looked up from his bag.

'Hullo, Allen,' he said, 'what the dickens are you up here for?'

'I was rather thinking of doing a little boxing. If you've no objection, of course.'

'But you ought to be on a bed of sickness, and that sort of thing. I heard you'd crocked yourself.'

'So I did. Nothing much, though. Trod on myself during a game of fives, and twisted my ankle a bit.'

'In for the middles, of course?'

'Yes.'

'So am I.'

'Yes, so I saw in the *Sportsman*. It says you weigh eleven-three.'

'Bit more, really, I believe. Shan't be able to have any lunch, or I shall have to go in for the heavies. What are you?'

'Just eleven. Well, let's hope we meet in the final.'

'Rather,' said Tony.

It was at Aldershot – to be more exact, in the dressing-room of the Queen's Avenue Gymnasium at Aldershot – that the conversation took place. From east and west, and north and south, from Dan even unto Beersheba, the representatives of the public schools had assembled to box, fence, and perform gymnastic prodigies for fame and silver medals. The room was full of all sorts and sizes of them, heavy-weights looking ponderous and muscular, feather-weights diminutive but wiry, light-weights, middle-weights, fencers, and gymnasts in scores, some wearing the unmistakable air of the veteran, for whom Aldershot has no mysteries, others nervous, and wishing themselves back again at school.

Tony Graham had chosen a corner near the door. This was his first appearance at Aldershot. St Austin's was his School, and he was by far the best middle-weight there. But his doubts as to his ability to hold his own against all-comers were extreme, nor were they lessened by the knowledge that his cousin, Allen Thomson, was to be one of his opponents. Indeed, if he had not been a man of mettle, he might well have thought that with Allen's advent his chances were at an end.

Allen was at Rugby. He was the son of a baronet who owned many acres in Wiltshire, and held fixed opinions on the subject of the whole duty of man, who, he held, should be before anything else a sportsman. Both the Thomsons – Allen's brother Jim was at St Austin's in the same House as Tony – were good at most forms of sport. Jim, however, had never taken to the art of boxing very kindly, but, by way of compensation, Allen had skill enough for two. He was a splendid boxer, quick, neat, scientific. He had been up to Aldershot three times, once as a feather-weight and twice as a light-weight, and each time he had returned with the silver medal.

As for Tony, he was more a fighter than a sparrer. When he paid a visit to his uncle's house he boxed with Allen daily, and invariably got the worst of it. Allen was too quick for him. But he was clever with his hands. His supply of pluck was inexhaustible, and physically he was as hard as nails.

'Is your ankle all right again, now?' he asked.

'Pretty well. It wasn't much of a sprain. Interfered with my training a good bit, though. I ought by rights to be well under eleven stone. You're all right, I suppose?'

'Not bad. Boxing takes it out of you more than footer or a race. I was in good footer training long before I started to get fit for Aldershot. But I think I ought to get along fairly well. Any idea who's in against us?'

'Harrow, Felsted, Wellington. That's all, I think.'

'St Paul's?'

'No.'

'Good. Well, I hope your first man mops you up. I've a conscientious objection to scrapping with you.'

Allen laughed. 'You'd be all right,' he said, 'if you weren't so beastly slow with your guard. Why don't you wake up? You hit like blazes.'

'I think I shall start guarding two seconds before you lead. By the way, don't have any false delicacy about spoiling my aristocratic features. On the ground of relationship, you know.'

'Rather not. Let auld acquaintance be forgot. I'm not Thomson for the present. I'm Rugby.'

'Just so, and I'm St Austin's. Personally, I'm going for the knock-out. You won't feel hurt?'

This was in the days before the Headmasters' Conference had abolished the knock-out blow, and a boxer might still pay attentions to the point of his opponent's jaw with an easy conscience.

'I probably shall if it comes off,' said Allen. 'I say, it occurs to me that we shall be weighing-in in a couple of minutes, and I haven't started to change yet. Good, I've not brought evening dress or somebody else's footer clothes, as usually happens on these festive occasions.'

He was just pulling on his last boot when a Gymnasium official appeared in the doorway.

'Will all those who are entering for the boxing get ready for the weighing-in, please?' he said, and a general exodus ensued.

The weighing-in at the Public Schools' Boxing Competition is something in the nature of a religious ceremony, but even religious ceremonies come to an end, and after a quarter of an hour or so Tony was weighed in the balance and found correct. He strolled off on a tour of inspection.

After a time he lighted upon the St Austin's Gym Instructor, whom he had not seen since they had parted that morning, the one on his way to the dressing-room, the other to the refreshment-bar for a modest quencher.

'Well, Mr Graham?'

'Hullo, Dawkins. What time does this show start? Do you know when the middle-weights come on?'

'Well, you can't say for certain. They may keep 'em back a bit or they may make a start with 'em first thing. No, the light-weights are going to start. What number did you draw, sir?'

'One.'

'Then you'll be in the first middle-weight pair. That'll be after these two gentlemen.'

'These two gentlemen', the first of the light-weights, were by this time in the middle of a warmish opening round. Tony watched them with interest and envy. 'How beastly nippy they are,' he said.

'Wish I could duck like that,' he added.

'Well, the 'ole thing there is you 'ave to watch the other man's eyes. But light-weights is always quicker at the duck than what heavier men are. You get the best boxing in the light-weights, though the feathers spar quicker.'

Soon afterwards the contest finished, amidst volleys of applause. It had been a spirited battle, and an exceedingly close thing. The umpires disagreed. After a short consultation, the referee gave it as his opinion that on the whole R. Cloverdale, of Bedford, had had a shade the worse of the exchanges, and that in consequence J. Robinson, of St Paul's, was the victor. This was what he meant. What he said was, 'Robinson wins,' in a sharp voice, as if somebody were arguing about it. The pair then shook hands and retired.

'First bout, middle-weights,' shrilled the M.C. 'W. P. Ross (Wellington) and A. C. R. Graham (St Austin's).'

Tony and his opponent retired for a moment to the changing-room, and then made their way amidst applause on to the raised stage on which the ring was pitched. Mr W. P. Ross proceeded to the farther corner of the ring, where he sat down and was vigorously massaged by his two seconds. Tony took the opposite corner and submitted himself to the same process. It is a very cheering thing at any time to have one's arms and legs kneaded like bread, and it is especially pleasant if one is at all nervous. It sends a glow through the entire frame. Like somebody's something it is both grateful and comforting.

Tony's seconds were curious specimens of humanity. One was a gigantic soldier, very gruff and taciturn, and with decided leanings towards pessimism. The other was also a soldier. He was in every way his colleague's opposite. He was half his size, had red hair, and was bubbling over with conversation. The other could not interfere with his hair or his size, but he could with his conversation, and whenever he attempted a remark, he was promptly silenced, much to his disgust.

'Plenty o' moosle 'ere, Fred,' he began, as he rubbed Tony's left arm.

'Moosle ain't everything,' said the other, gloomily, and there was silence again.

'Are you ready? Seconds away,' said the referee.

'Time!'

The two stood up to one another.

The Wellington representative was a plucky boxer, but he was not in the same class as Tony. After a few exchanges, the latter got to work, and after that there was only one man in the ring. In the middle of the second round the referee stopped the fight, and gave it to Tony, who came away as fresh as he had started, and a great deal happier and more confident.

'Did us proud, Fred,' began the garrulous man.

'Yes, but that 'un ain't nothing. You wait till he meets young Thomson. I've seen 'im box 'ere three years, and never bin beat yet. Three bloomin' years. Yus.'

This might have depressed anybody else, but as Tony already knew all there was to be known about Allen's skill with the gloves, it had no effect upon him.

A sanguinary heavy-weight encounter was followed by the first bout of the feathers and the second of the light-weights, and then it was Allen's turn to fight the Harrow representative.

It was not a very exciting bout. Allen took things very easily. He knew his training was by no means all it should have been, and it was not his game to take it out of himself with any firework business in the trial heats. He would reserve that for the final. So he sparred three gentle rounds with the Harrow sportsman, just doing sufficient to keep the lead and obtain the verdict after the last round. He finished without having turned a hair. He had only received one really hard blow, and that had done no damage. After this came a long series of fights. The heavy-weights shed their blood in gallons for name and fame. The feather-weights gave excellent exhibitions of science, and the light-weight pairs were fought off until there remained only the final to be decided, Robinson, of St Paul's, against a Charterhouse boxer.

In the middle-weights there were three competitors still in the running, Allen, Tony, and a Felsted man. They drew lots, and the bye fell to Tony, who put up an uninteresting three rounds with one of the soldiers, neither fatiguing himself very much. Henderson, of Felsted, proved a much tougher nut to crack than Allen's first opponent. He was a rushing boxer, and in the first round had, if anything, the best of it. In the last two, however, Allen gradually forged ahead, gaining many points by his perfect style alone. He was declared the winner, but he felt much more tired than he had done after his first fight.

By the time he was required again, however, he had had plenty of breathing space. The final of the light-weights had been decided, and Robinson, of St Paul's, after the custom of Paulines, had set the crown upon his afternoon's work by fighting the Carthusian to a standstill in the first round. There only remained now the finals of the heavies and middles.

It was decided to take the latter first.

Tony had his former seconds, and Dawkins had come to his corner to see him through the ordeal.

'The 'ole thing 'ere,' he kept repeating, 'is to keep goin' 'ard all the time and wear 'im out. He's too quick for you to try any sparrin' with.'

'Yes,' said Tony.

'The 'ole thing,' continued the expert, 'is to feint with your left and 'it with your right.' This was excellent in theory, no doubt, but Tony felt that when he came to put it into practice Allen might have other schemes on hand and bring them off first.

'Are you ready? Seconds out of the ring . . . Time!'

'Go in, sir, 'ard,' whispered the red-haired man as Tony rose from his place.

Allen came up looking pleased with matters in general. He gave Tony a cousinly grin as they shook hands. Tony did not respond. He was feeling serious, and wondering if he could bring off his knock-out before the three rounds were over. He had his doubts.

The fight opened slowly. Both were cautious, for each knew the other's powers. Suddenly, just as Tony was thinking of leading, Allen came in like a flash. A straight left between the eyes, a right on the side of the head, and a second left on the exact tip of the nose, and he was out again, leaving Tony with a helpless feeling of impotence and disgust.

Then followed more sparring. Tony could never get in exactly the right position for a rush. Allen circled round him with an occasional feint. Then he hit out with the left. Tony ducked. Again he hit, and again Tony ducked, but this time the left stopped halfway, and his right caught Tony on the cheek just as he swayed to one side. It staggered him, and before he could recover himself, in darted Allen again with another trio of blows, ducked a belated left counter, got in two stinging hits on the ribs, and finished with a left drive which took Tony clean off his feet and deposited him on the floor beside the ropes.

'Silence, *please*,' said the referee, as a burst of applause greeted this feat.

Tony was up again in a moment. He began to feel savage. He had expected something like this, but that gave him no consolation. He made up his mind that he really would rush this time, but just as he was coming in, Allen came in instead. It seemed to Tony for the next half-minute that his cousin's fists were never out of his face. He looked on the world through a brown haze of boxing-glove. Occasionally his hand met something solid which he took to be Allen, but this was seldom, and, whenever it happened, it only seemed to bring him back again like a boomerang. Just at the most exciting point, 'Time' was called.

The pessimist shook his head gloomily as he sponged Tony's face.

'You must lead if you want to 'it 'im,' said the garrulous man. 'You're too slow. Go in at 'im, sir, wiv both 'ands, an' you'll be all right. Won't 'e, Fred?'

'I said 'ow it 'ud be,' was the only reply Fred would vouchsafe.

Tony was half afraid the referee would give the fight against him without another round, but to his joy 'Time' was duly called. He came up to the scratch as game as ever, though his head was singing. He meant to go in for all he was worth this round.

And go in he did. Allen had managed, in performing a complicated manoeuvre, to place himself in a corner, and Tony rushed. He was sent out again with a flush hit on the face. He rushed again, and again met Allen's left. Then he got past, and in the confined space had it all his own way. Science did not tell here. Strength was the thing that scored, hard half-arm smashes, left and right, at face and body, and the guard could look after itself.

Allen upper-cut him twice, but after that he was nowhere. Tony went in with both hands. There was a prolonged rally, and it was not until 'Time' had been called that Allen was able to extricate himself. Tony's blows had been mostly body blows, and very warm ones at that.

'That's right, sir,' was the comment of the red-headed second. 'Keep 'em both goin' hard, and you'll win yet. You 'ad 'im proper then. 'Adn't 'e, Fred?'

And even the pessimist was obliged to admit that Tony could fight, even if he was not quick with his guard.

Allen took the ring slowly. His want of training had begun to tell on him, and some of Tony's blows had landed in very tender spots. He knew that he could win if his wind held out, but he had misgivings. The gloves seemed to weigh down his hands. Tony opened the ball with a tremendous rush. Allen stopped him neatly. There was an interval while the two sparred for an opening. Then Allen feinted and dashed in. Tony did not hit him once. It was the first round over again. Left right, left right, and, finally, as had happened before, a tremendously hot shot which sent him under the ropes. He got up, and again Allen darted in. Tony met him with a straight left. A rapid exchange of blows, and the end came. Allen lashed out with his left. Tony ducked sharply, and brought his right across with every ounce of his weight behind it, fairly on to the point of the jaw. The right cross-counter is distinctly one of those things which it is more blessed to give than to receive. Allen collapsed.

'... nine ... ten.'

The time-keeper closed his watch.

'Graham wins,' said the referee, 'look after that man there.'

2 THIEVES BREAK IN AND STEAL

It was always the custom for such Austinians as went up to represent the School at the annual competition to stop the night in the town. It was not, therefore, till just before breakfast on the following day that Tony arrived back at his House. The boarding Houses at St Austin's formed a fringe to the School grounds. The two largest were the School House and Merevale's. Tony was at Merevale's. He was walking up from the station with Welch, another member of Merevale's, who had been up to Aldershot as a fencer, when, at the entrance to the School grounds, he fell in with Robinson, his fag. Robinson was supposed by many (including himself) to be a very warm man for the Junior Quarter, which was a handicap race, especially as an injudicious Sports Committee had given him ten yards' start on Simpson, whom he would have backed himself to beat, even if the positions had been reversed. Being a wise youth, however, and knowing that the best of runners may fail through under-training, he had for the last week or so been going in for a steady course of over-training, getting up in the small hours and going for before-breakfast spins round the track on a glass of milk and a piece of bread. Master R. Robinson was nothing if not thorough in matters of this kind.

But today things of greater moment than the Sports occupied

his mind. He had news. He had great news. He was bursting with news, and he hailed the approach of Tony and Welch with pleasure. With any other leading light of the School he might have felt less at ease, but with Tony it was different. When you have underdone a fellow's eggs and overdone his toast and eaten the remainder for a term or two, you begin to feel that mere social distinctions and differences of age no longer form a barrier.

Besides, he had news which was absolutely fresh, news to which no one could say pityingly: 'What! Have you only just heard *that*!'

'Hullo, Graham,' he said. 'Have you come back?' Tony admitted that he had. 'Jolly good for getting the Middles.' (A telegram had, of course, preceded Tony.) 'I say, Graham, do you know what's happened? There'll be an awful row about it. Someone's been and broken into the Pav.'

'Rot! How do you know?'

'There's a pane taken clean out. I booked it in a second as I was going past to the track.'

'Which room?'

'First Fifteen. The window facing away from the Houses.'

'That's rum,' said Welch. 'Wonder what a burglar wanted in the First room. Isn't even a hair-brush there generally.'

Robinson's eyes dilated with honest pride. This was good. This was better than he had looked for. Not only were they unaware of the burglary, but they had not even an idea as to the recent event which had made the First room so fit a hunting-ground for the burgling industry. There are few pleasures keener than the pleasure of telling somebody something he didn't know before.

'Great Scott,' he remarked, 'haven't you heard? No, of course you went up to Aldershot before they did it. By Jove.'

'Did what?'

'Why, they shunted all the Sports prizes from the Board Room to the Pav. and shot 'em into the First room. I don't suppose there's one left now. I should like to see the Old Man's face when he hears about it. Good mind to go and tell him now, only he'd have a fit. Jolly exciting, though, isn't it?'

'Well,' said Tony, 'of all the absolutely idiotic things to do! Fancy putting – there must have been at least fifty pounds' worth of silver and things. Fancy going and leaving all that overnight in the Pav.!'

'Rotten!' agreed Welch. 'Wonder whose idea it was.'

'Look here, Robinson,' said Tony, 'you'd better buck up and change, or you'll be late for brekker. Come on, Welch, we'll go and inspect the scene of battle.'

Robinson trotted off, and Welch and Tony made their way to the Pavilion. There, sure enough, was the window, or rather the absence of window. A pane had been neatly removed, evidently in the orthodox way by means of a diamond.

'May as well climb up and see if there's anything to be seen,' said Welch.

'All right,' said Tony, 'give us a leg up. Right-ho. By Jove, I'm stiff.'

'See anything?'

'No. There's a cloth sort of thing covering what I suppose are the prizes. I see how the chap, whoever he was, got in. You've only got to break the window, draw a couple of bolts, and there you are. Shall I go in and investigate?'

'Better not. It's rather the thing, I fancy, in these sorts of cases, to leave everything just as it is.'

'Rum business,' said Tony, as he rejoined Welch on terra firma. 'Wonder if they'll catch the chap. We'd better be getting back to the House now. It struck the quarter years ago.'

When Tony, some twenty minutes later, shook off the admiring crowd who wanted a full description of yesterday's proceedings, and reached his study, he found there James Thomson, brother to Allen Thomson, as the playbills say. Jim was looking worried. Tony had noticed it during breakfast, and had wondered at the cause. He was soon enlightened.

'Hullo, Jim,' said he. 'What's up with you this morning? Feeling chippy?'

'No. No, I'm all right. I'm in a beastly hole though. I wanted to talk to you about it.'

'Weigh in, then. We've got plenty of time before school.'

'It's about this Aldershot business. How on earth did you manage to lick Allen like that? I thought he was a cert.'

'Yes, so did I. The 'ole thing there, as Dawkins 'ud say, was, I knocked him out. It's the sort of thing that's always happening. I wasn't in it at all except during the second round, when I gave him beans rather in one of the corners. My aunt, it was warm while it lasted. First round, I didn't hit him once. He was better than I thought he'd be, and I knew from experience he was pretty good.'

'Yes, you look a bit bashed.'

'Yes. Feel it too. But what's the row with you?'

'Just this. I had a couple of quid on Allen, and the rotter goes and gets licked.'

'Good Lord. Whom did you bet with?'

'With Allen himself.'

'Mean to say Allen was crock enough to bet against himself? He must have known he was miles better than anyone else in. He's got three medals there already.'

'No, you see his bet with me was only a hedge. He'd got five to four or something in quids on with a chap in his House at

Rugby on himself. He wanted a hedge because he wasn't sure about his ankle being all right. You know he hurt it. So I gave him four to one in half-sovereigns. I thought he was a cert, with apologies to you.'

'Don't mention it. So he was a cert. It was only the merest fluke I managed to out him when I did. If he'd hung on to the end, he'd have won easy. He'd been scoring points all through.'

'I know. So the *Sportsman* says. Just like my luck.'

'I can't see what you want to bet at all for. You're bound to come a mucker sooner or later. Can't you raise the two quid?'

'I'm broke except for half a crown.'

'I'd lend it to you like a shot if I had it, of course. But you don't find me with two quid to my name at the end of term. Won't Allen wait?'

'He would if it was only him. But this other chap wants his oof badly for something and he's leaving and going abroad or something at the end of term. Anyhow, I know he's keen on getting it. Allen told me.'

Tony pondered for a moment. 'Look here,' he said at last, 'can't you ask your pater? He usually heaves his money about pretty readily, doesn't he?'

'Well, you see, he wouldn't send me two quid off the reel without wanting to know all about it, and why I couldn't get on to the holidays with five bob, and I'd either have to fake up a lot of lies, which I'm not going to do—'

'Of course not.'

'Or else I must tell him I've been betting.'

'Well, he bets himself, doesn't he?'

'That's just where the whole business slips up,' replied Jim, prodding the table with a pen in a misanthropic manner. 'Betting's the one thing he's absolutely down on. He got done rather badly once a few years ago. Believe he betted on Orme that year he got poisoned. Anyhow he's always sworn to lynch us if we made fools of ourselves that way. So if I asked him, I'd not only get beans myself, besides not getting any money out of him, but Allen would get scalped too, which he wouldn't see at all.'

'Yes, it's no good doing that. Haven't you any other source of revenue?'

'Yes, there's just one chance. If that doesn't come off, I'm done. My pater said he'd give me a quid for every race I won at the sports. I got the half yesterday all right when you were up at Aldershot.'

'Good man. I didn't hear about that. What time? Anything good?'

'Nothing special. 2 – 7 and three-fifths.'

'That's awfully good. You ought to pull off the mile, too, I should think.'

'Yes, with luck. Drake's the man I'm afraid of. He's done it in 4 – 48 twice during training. He was second in the half yesterday by about three yards, but you can't tell anything from that. He sprinted too late.'

'What's your best for the mile?'

'I have done 4 – 47, but only once. 4 – 48's my average, so there's nothing to choose between us on paper.'

'Well, you've got more to make you buck up than he has. There must be something in that.'

'Yes, by Jove. I'll win if I expire on the tape. I shan't spare myself with that quid on the horizon.'

'No. Hullo, there's the bell. We must buck up. Going to Charteris' gorge tonight?'

'Yes, but I shan't eat anything. No risks for me.'

'Rusks are more in your line now. Come on.'

And, in the excitement of these more personal matters, Tony entirely forgot to impart the news of the Pavilion burglary to him.

3 AN UNIMPORTANT BY-PRODUCT

The news, however, was not long in spreading. Robinson took care of that. On the way to school he overtook his friend Morrison, a young gentleman who had the unique distinction of being the rowdiest fag in Ward's House, which, as any Austinian could have told you, was the rowdiest house in the School.

'I say, Morrison, heard the latest?'

'No, what?'

'Chap broke into the Pav. last night.'

'Who, you?'

'No, you ass, a regular burglar. After the Sports prizes.'

'Look here, Robinson, try that on the kids.'

'Just what I am doing,' said Robinson.

This delicate reference to Morrison's tender years had the effect of creating a disturbance. Two School House juniors, who happened to be passing, naturally forsook all their other aims and objects and joined the battle.

'What's up?' asked one of them, dusting himself hastily as they stopped to take breath. It was always his habit to take up any business that might attract his attention, and ask for explanations afterwards.

'This kid—' began Morrison.

'Kid yourself, Morrison.'

'This lunatic, then.' Robinson allowed the emendation to pass. 'This lunatic's got some yarn on about the Pav. being burgled.'

'So it is. Tell you I saw it myself.'

'Did it yourself, probably.'

'How do you know, anyway? You seem so jolly certain about it.'

'Why, there's a pane of glass cut out of the window in the First room.'

'Shouldn't wonder, you know,' said Dimsdale, one of the two School House fags, judicially, 'if the kid wasn't telling the truth for once in his life. Those pots must be worth something. Don't you think so, Scott?'

Scott admitted that there might be something in the idea, and that, however foreign to his usual habits, Robinson might on this occasion be confining himself more or less to strict fact.

'There you are, then,' said Robinson, vengefully. 'Shows what a fat lot you know what you're talking about, Morrison.'

'Morrison's a fool,' said Scott. 'Ever since he got off the bottom bench in form there's been no holding him.'

'All the same,' said Morrison, feeling that matters were going against him, 'I shan't believe it till I see it.'

'What'll you bet?' said Robinson.

'I never bet,' replied Morrison with scorn.

'You daren't. You know you'd lose.'

'All right, then, I'll bet a penny I'm right.' He drew a deep breath, as who should say, 'It's a lot of money, but it's worth risking it.'

'You'll lose that penny, old chap,' said Robinson. 'That's to say,' he added thoughtfully, 'if you ever pay up.'

'You've got us as witnesses,' said Dimsdale. 'We'll see that he shells out. Scott, remember you're a witness.'

'Right-ho,' said Scott.

At this moment the clock struck nine, and as each of the principals in this financial transaction, and both the witnesses, were expected to be in their places to answer their names at 8.58, they were late. And as they had all been late the day before and the day before that, they were presented with two hundred lines apiece. Which shows more than ever how wrong it is to bet.

The news continuing to circulate, by the end of morning school it was generally known that a gang of desperadoes, numbering at least a hundred, had taken the Pavilion down, brick by brick, till only the foundations were left standing, and had gone off with every jot and tittle of the unfortunately placed Sports prizes.

At the quarter-to-eleven interval, the School had gone *en masse* to see what it could see, and had stared at the window with much the same interest as they were wont to use in inspecting the First Eleven pitch on the morning of a match – a curious custom, by the way, but one very generally observed.

Then the official news of the extent of the robbery was spread abroad. It appeared that the burglar had by no means done the profession credit, for out of a vast collection of prizes ranging from the vast and silver Mile Challenge Cup to the pair of fives-gloves with which the 'under twelve' disciple of Deerfoot was to be rewarded, he had selected only three. Two of these were worth having, being the challenge cup for the quarter and the non-challenge cup for the hundred yards, both silver, but the third was a valueless flask, and the general voice of the School was loud in condemning the business abilities of one who could select his swag in so haphazard a manner. It was felt to detract from the merit of the performance. The knowing ones, however, gave it as their opinion that the man must have been frightened by something, and so was unable to give the matter his best attention and do himself justice as a connoisseur.

'We had a burglary at my place once,' began Reade, of Philpott's House. 'The man—'

'That rotter, Reade,' said Barrett, also of Philpott's, 'has been telling us that burglary chestnut of his all the morning. I wish you chaps wouldn't encourage him.'

'Why, what was it? First I've heard of it, at any rate.' Dallas and Vaughan, of Ward's, added themselves to the group. 'Out with it, Reade,' said Vaughan.

'It's only a beastly reminiscence of Reade's childhood,' said Barrett. 'A burglar got into the wine-cellar and collared all the coals.'

'He didn't. He was in the hall, and my pater got his revolver—'

'While you hid under the bed.'

'—and potted at him over the banisters.'

'The last time but three you told the story, your pater fired through the keyhole of the dining-room.'

'You idiot, that was afterwards.'

'Oh, well, what does it matter? Tell us something fresh.'

'It's my opinion,' said Dallas, 'that Ward did it. A man of the vilest antecedents. He's capable of anything from burglary—'

'To attempted poisoning. You should see what we get to eat in Ward's House,' said Vaughan.

'Ward's the worst type of beak. He simply lives for the sake of booking chaps. If he books a chap out of bounds it keeps him happy for a week.'

'A man like that's bound to be a criminal of sorts in his spare time. It's action and reaction,' said Vaughan.

Mr Ward happening to pass at this moment, the speaker went on to ask Dallas audibly if life was worth living, and Dallas replied that under certain conditions and in some Houses it was not.

Dallas and Vaughan did not like Mr Ward. Mr Ward was not the sort of man who inspires affection. He had an unpleasant habit of 'jarring', as it was called. That is to say, his conversation was shaped to one single end, that of trying to make the person to whom he talked feel uncomfortable. Many of his jars had become part of the School history. There was a legend that on one occasion he had invited his prefects to supper, and regaled them with sausages. There was still one prefect unhelped. To him he addressed himself.

'A sausage, Jones?'

'If you please, sir.'

'No, you won't, then, because I'm going to have half myself.'

This story may or may not be true. Suffice it to say, that Mr Ward was not popular.

The discussion was interrupted by the sound of the bell ringing for second lesson. The problem was left unsolved. It was evident that the burglar had been interrupted, but how or why nobody knew. The suggestion that he had heard Master R. Robinson training for his quarter-mile, and had thought it was an earthquake, found much favour with the junior portion of the assembly. Simpson, on whom Robinson had been given start in the race, expressed an opinion that he, Robinson, ran like a cow. At which Robinson smiled darkly, and advised the other to wait till Sports Day and then he'd see, remarking that, meanwhile, if he gave him any of his cheek he might not be well enough to run at all.

'This sort of thing,' said Barrett to Reade, as they walked to their form-room, 'always makes me feel beastly. Once start a row like this, and all the beaks turn into regular detectives and go ferreting about all over the place, and it's ten to one they knock up against something one doesn't want them to know about.'

Reade was feeling hurt. He had objected to the way in which Barrett had spoiled a story that might easily have been true, and really was true in parts. His dignity was offended. He said 'Yes' to Barrett's observation in a tone of reserved *hauteur*. Barrett did not notice.

'It's an awful nuisance. For one thing it makes them so jolly strict about bounds.'

'Yes.'

'I wanted to go for a bike ride this afternoon. There's nothing on at the School.'

'Why don't you?'

'What's the good if you can't break bounds? A ride of about a quarter of a mile's no good. There's a ripping place about ten miles down the Stapleton Road. Big wood, with a ripping little hollow in the middle, all ferns and moss. I was thinking of taking a book out there for the afternoon. Only there's roll-call.'

He paused. Ordinarily, this would have been the cue for Reade to say, 'Oh, I'll answer your name at roll-call.' But Reade said nothing. Barrett looked surprised and disappointed.

'I say, Reade,' he said.

'Well?'

'Would you like to answer my name at roll-call?' It was the first time he had ever had occasion to make the request.

'No,' said Reade.

Barrett could hardly believe his ears. Did he sleep? Did he dream? Or were visions about?

'What!' he said.

No answer.

'Do you mean to say you won't?'

'Of course I won't. Why the deuce should I do your beastly dirty work for you?'

Barrett did not know what to make of this. Curiosity urged him to ask for explanations. Dignity threw cold water on such a scheme. In the end dignity had the best of it.

'Oh, very well,' he said, and they went on in silence. In all the three years of their acquaintance they had never before happened upon such a crisis.

The silence lasted until they reached the form-room. Then Barrett determined, in the interests of the common good – he and Reade shared a study, and icy coolness in a small study is unpleasant – to chain up Dignity for the moment, and give Curiosity a trial.

'What's up with you today?' he asked.

He could hardly have chosen a worse formula. The question has on most people precisely the same effect as that which the query, 'Do you know where you lost it?' has on one who is engaged in looking for mislaid property.

'Nothing,' said Reade. Probably at the same moment hundreds of other people were making the same reply, in the same tone of voice, to the same question.

'Oh,' said Barrett.

There was another silence.

'You might as well answer my name this afternoon,' said Barrett, tentatively.

Reade walked off without replying, and Barrett went to his place feeling that curiosity was a fraud, and resolving to confine his attentions for the future to dignity. This was by-product number one of the Pavilion burglary.

4 CERTAIN REVELATIONS

During the last hour of morning school, Tony got a note from Jim.

'Graham,' said Mr Thompson, the master of the Sixth, sadly, just as Tony was about to open it.

'Yes, sir?'

'Kindly tear that note up, Graham.'

'Note, sir?'

'Kindly tear that note up, Graham. Come, you are keeping us waiting.'

As the hero of the novel says, further concealment was useless. Tony tore the note up unread.

'Hope it didn't want an answer,' he said to Jim after school. 'Constant practice has made Thompson a sort of amateur lynx.'

'No. It was only to ask you to be in the study directly after lunch. There's a most unholy row going to occur shortly, as far as I can see.'

'What, about this burglary business?'

'Yes. Haven't time to tell you now. See you after lunch.'

After lunch, having closed the study door, Jim embarked on the following statement.

It appeared that on the previous night he had left a book of notes, which were of absolutely vital importance for the examination which the Sixth had been doing in the earlier part of the morning, in the identical room in which the prizes had been placed. Or rather, he had left it there several days before, and had not needed it till that night. At half-past six the Pavilion had been locked up, and Biffen, the ground-man, had taken the key away with him, and it was only after tea had been consumed and the evening paper read, that Jim, thinking it about time to begin work, had discovered his loss. This was about half-past seven.

Being a House-prefect, Jim did not attend preparation in the Great Hall with the common herd of the Houses, but was part-owner with Tony of a study.

The difficulties of the situation soon presented themselves to him. It was only possible to obtain the notes in three ways – firstly, by going to the rooms of the Sixth Form master, who lived out of College; secondly, by borrowing from one of the other Sixth Form members of the House; and thirdly, by the desperate expedient of burgling the Pavilion. The objections to the first course were two. In the first place Merevale was taking prep. over in the Hall, and it was strictly forbidden for anyone to quit the House after lock-up without leave. And, besides, it was long odds that Thompson, the Sixth Form master, would not have the notes, as he had dictated them partly out of his head and partly from the works of various eminent scholars. The second course was out of the question. The only other Sixth Form boy in the House, Tony and Welch being away at Aldershot, was Charteris, and Charteris, who never worked much except the night before an exam. but worked then under forced draught, was appalled at the mere suggestion of letting his note-book out of his hands. Jim had sounded him on the subject and had met with the reply, 'Kill my father and burn my ancestral home, and

I will look on and smile. But touch these notes and you rouse the British Lion.' After which he had given up the borrowing idea.

There remained the third course, and there was an excitement and sporting interest about it that took him immensely. But how was he to get out to start with? He opened his study-window and calculated the risks of a drop to the ground. No, it was too far. Not worth risking a sprained ankle on the eve of the mile. Then he thought of the Matron's sitting-room. This was on the ground-floor, and if its owner happened to be out, exit would be easy. As luck would have it she was out, and in another minute Jim had crossed the Rubicon and was standing on the gravel drive which led to the front gate.

A sharp sprint took him to the Pavilion. Now the difficulty was not how to get out, but how to get in. Theoretically, it should have been the easiest of tasks, but in practice there were plenty of obstacles to success. He tried the lower windows, but they were firmly fixed. There had been a time when one of them would yield to a hard kick and fly bodily out of its frame, but somebody had been caught playing that game not long before, and Jim remembered with a pang that not only had the window been securely fastened up, but the culprit had had a spell of extra tuition and other punishments which had turned him for the time into a hater of his species. His own fate, he knew, would be even worse, for a prefect is supposed to have something better to do in his spare time than breaking into pavilions. It would mean expulsion perhaps, or, at the least, the loss of his prefect's cap, and Jim did not want to lose that. Still the thing had to be done if he meant to score any marks at all in the forthcoming exam. He wavered a while between a choice of methods, and finally fixed on the crudest of all. No one was likely to be within earshot, thought he, so he picked up the largest stone he could find, took as careful aim as the dim light would allow, and hove it. There was a sickening crash, loud enough, he thought, to bring the whole School down on him, followed by a prolonged rattle as the broken pieces of glass fell to the ground.

He held his breath and listened. For a moment all was still, uncannily still. He could hear the tops of the trees groaning in the slight breeze that had sprung up, and far away the distant roar of a train. Then a queer thing happened. He heard a quiet thud, as if somebody had jumped from a height on to grass, and then quick footsteps.

He waited breathless and rigid, expecting every moment to see a form loom up beside him in the darkness. It was useless to run. His only chance was to stay perfectly quiet.

Then it dawned upon him that the man was running away from him, not towards him. His first impulse was to give chase, but prudence restrained him. Catching burglars is an exhilarating sport, but it is best to indulge in it when one is not on a burgling expedition oneself.

Besides he had come out to get his book, and business is business.

There was no time to be lost now, for someone might have heard one or both of the noises and given the alarm.

Once the window was broken the rest was fairly easy, the only danger being the pieces of glass. He took off his coat and flung it on to the sill of the upper window. In a few seconds he was up himself without injury. He found it a trifle hard to keep his balance, as there was nothing to hold on to, but he managed it long enough to enable him to thrust an arm through the gap and turn the handle. After this there was a bolt to draw, which he managed without difficulty.

The window swung open. Jim jumped in, and groped his way

round the room till he found his book. The other window of the room was wide open. He shut it for no definite reason, and noticed that a pane had been cut out entire. The professional cracksman had done his work more neatly than the amateur.

'Poor chap,' thought Jim, with a chuckle, as he effected a retreat, 'I must have given him a bit of a start with my half-brick.' After bolting the window behind him, he climbed down.

As he reached earth again the clock struck a quarter to nine. In another quarter of an hour prep. would be over and the House door unlocked, and he would be able to get in again. Nor would the fact of his being out excite remark, for it was the custom of the House-prefects to take the air for the few minutes which elapsed between the opening of the door and the final locking-up for the night.

The rest of his adventures ran too smoothly to require a detailed description. Everything succeeded excellently. The only reminiscences of his escapade were a few cuts in his coat, which went unnoticed, and the precious book of notes, to which he applied himself with such vigour in the watches of the night, with a surreptitious candle and a hamper of apples as aids to study, that, though tired next day, he managed to do quite well enough in the exam. to pass muster. And, as he had never had the least prospect of coming out top, or even in the first five, this satisfied him completely.

Tony listened with breathless interest to Jim's recital of his adventures, and at the conclusion laughed.

'What a mad thing to go and do,' he said. 'Jolly sporting, though.'

Jim did not join in his laughter.

'Yes, but don't you see,' he said, ruefully, 'what a mess I'm in? If they find out that I was in the Pav. at the time when the cups were bagged, how on earth am I to prove I didn't take them myself?'

'By Jove, I never thought of that. But, hang it all, they'd never dream of accusing a Coll. chap of stealing Sports prizes. This isn't a reformatory for juvenile hooligans.'

'No, perhaps not.'

'Of course not.'

'Well, even if they didn't, the Old Man would be frightfully sick if he got to know about it. I'd lose my prefect's cap for a cert.'

'You might, certainly.'

'I should. There wouldn't be any question about it. Why, don't you remember that business last summer about Cairns? He used to stay out after lock-up. That was absolutely all he did. Well, the Old 'Un dropped on him like a hundredweight of bricks. Multiply that by about ten and you get what he'll do to me if he books me over this job.'

Tony looked thoughtful. The case of Cairns *versus* The Powers that were, was too recent to have escaped his memory. Even now Cairns was to be seen on the grounds with a common School House cap at the back of his head in place of the prefect's cap which had once adorned it.

'Yes,' he said, 'you'd lose your cap all right, I'm afraid.'

'Rather. And the sickening part of the business is that this real, copper-bottomed burglary'll make them hunt about all over the shop for clues and things, and the odds are they'll find me out, even if they don't book the real man. Shouldn't wonder if they had a detective down for a big thing of this sort.'

'They are having one, I heard.'

'There you are, then,' said Jim, dejectedly. 'I'm done, you see.'

'I don't know. I don't believe detectives are much class.'

'Anyhow, he'll probably have gumption enough to spot me.'

Jim's respect for the abilities of our national sleuth-hounds was greater than Tony's, and a good deal greater than that of most people.

5 CONCERNING THE MUTUAL FRIEND

'I wonder where the dear Mutual gets to these afternoons,' said Dallas.

'The who?' asked MacArthur. MacArthur, commonly known as the Babe, was a day boy. Dallas and Vaughan had invited him to tea in their study.

'Plunkett, you know.'

'Why the Mutual?'

'Mutual Friend, Vaughan's and mine. Shares this study with us. I call him dear partly because he's head of the House, and therefore, of course, we respect and admire him.'

'And partly,' put in Vaughan, beaming at the Babe over a frying-pan full of sausages, 'partly because we love him so. Oh, he's a beauty.'

'No, but rotting apart,' said the Babe, 'what sort of a chap is he? I hardly know him by sight, even.'

'Should describe him roughly,' said Dallas, 'as a hopeless, forsaken unspeakable worm.'

'Understates it considerably,' remarked Vaughan. 'His manners are patronizing, and his customs beastly.'

'He wears spectacles, and reads Herodotus in the original Greek for pleasure.'

'He sneers at footer, and jeers at cricket. Croquet is his form, I should say. Should doubt, though, if he even plays that.'

'But why on earth,' said the Babe, 'do you have him in your study?'

Vaughan looked wildly and speechlessly at Dallas, who looked helplessly back at Vaughan.

'Don't, Babe, please!' said Dallas. 'You've no idea how a remark of that sort infuriates us. You surely don't suppose we'd have the man in the study if we could help it?'

'It's another instance of Ward at his worst,' said Vaughan. 'Have you never heard the story of the Mutual Friend's arrival?'

'No.'

'It was like this. At the beginning of this term I came back expecting to be head of this show. You see, Richards left at Christmas and I was next man in. Dallas and I had made all sorts of arrangements for having a good time. Well, I got back on the last evening of the holidays. When I got into this study, there was the man Plunkett sitting in the best chair, reading.'

'Probably reading Herodotus in the original Greek,' snorted Dallas.

'He didn't take the slightest notice of me. I stood in the doorway like Patience on a monument for about a quarter of an hour. Then I coughed. He took absolutely no notice. I coughed again, loud enough to crack the windows. Then I got tired of it, and said "Hullo". He did look up at that. "Hullo," he said, "you've got rather a nasty cough." I said "Yes", and waited for him to throw himself on my bosom and explain everything, you know.'

'Did he?' asked the Babe, deeply interested.

'Not a bit,' said Dallas, 'he – sorry, Vaughan, fire ahead.'

'He went on reading. After a bit I said I hoped he was fairly comfortable. He said he was. Conversation languished again. I made another shot. "Looking for anybody?" I said. "No," he said, "are you?" "No." "Then why the dickens should I be?"

he said. I didn't quite follow his argument. In fact, I don't even now. "Look here," I said, "tell me one thing. Have you or have you not bought this place? If you have, all right. If you haven't, I'm going to sling you out, and jolly soon, too." He looked at me in his superior sort of way, and observed without blenching that he was head of the House.'

'Just another of Ward's jars,' said Dallas. 'Knowing that Vaughan was keen on being head of the House he actually went to the Old Man and persuaded him that it would be better to bring in some day boy who was a School-prefect than let Vaughan boss the show. What do you think of that?'

'Pretty low,' said the Babe.

'Said I was thoughtless and headstrong,' cut in Vaughan, spearing a sausage as if it were Mr Ward's body. 'Muffins up, Dallas, old man. When the sausages are done to a turn. "Thoughtless and headstrong." Those were his very words.'

'Can't you imagine the old beast?' said Dallas, pathetically. 'Can't you see him getting round the Old Man? A capital lad at heart, I am sure, distinctly a capital lad, but thoughtless and headstrong, far too thoughtless for a position so important as that of head of my House. The abandoned old wreck!'

Tea put an end for the moment to conversation, but when the last sausage had gone the way of all flesh, Vaughan returned to the sore subject like a moth to a candle.

'It isn't only the not being head of the House that I bar. It's the man himself. You say you haven't studied Plunkett much. When you get to know him better, you'll appreciate his finer qualities more. There are so few of them.'

'The only fine quality I've ever seen in him,' said Dallas, 'is his habit of slinking off in the afternoons when he ought to be playing games, and not coming back till lock-up.'

'Which brings us back to where we started,' put in the Babe. 'You were wondering what he did with himself.'

'Yes, it can't be anything good so we'll put beetles and butterflies out of the question right away. He might go and poach. There's heaps of opportunity round here for a chap who wants to try his hand at that. I remember, when I was a kid, Morton-Smith, who used to be in this House – remember him? – took me to old what's-his-name's place. Who's that frantic blood who owns all that land along the Badgwick road? The M.P. man.'

'Milord Sir Alfred Venner, M.P., of Badgwick Hall.'

'That's the man. Generally very much of Badgwick Hall. Came down last summer on Prize Day. One would have thought from the side on him that he was all sorts of dooks. Anyhow, Morton-Smith took me rabbiting there. I didn't know it was against the rules or anything. Had a grand time. A few days afterwards, Milord Sir Venner copped him on the hop and he got sacked. There was an awful row. I thought my hair would have turned white.'

'I shouldn't think the Mutual poaches,' said Vaughan. 'He hasn't got the enterprise to poach an egg even. No, it can't be that.'

'Perhaps he bikes?' said the Babe.

'No, he's not got a bike. He's the sort of chap, though, to borrow somebody else's without asking. Possibly he does bike.'

'If he does,' said Dallas, 'it's only so as to get well away from the Coll., before starting on his career of crime. I'll swear he does break rules like an ordinary human being when he thinks it's safe. Those aggressively pious fellows generally do.'

'I didn't know he was that sort,' said the Babe. 'Don't you find it rather a jar?'

'Just a bit. He jaws us sometimes till we turn and rend him.'

'Yes, he's an awful man,' said Vaughan.

'Don't stop,' said the Babe, encouragingly, after the silence had lasted some time. 'It's a treat picking a fellow to pieces like this.'

'I don't know if that's your beastly sarcasm, Babe,' said Vaughan, 'but, speaking for self and partner, I don't know how we should get on if we didn't blow off steam occasionally in this style.'

'We should probably last out for a week, and then there would be a sharp shriek, a hollow groan, and all that would be left of the Mutual Friend would be a slight discolouration on the study carpet.'

'Coupled with an aroma of fresh gore.'

'Perhaps that's why he goes off in the afternoons,' suggested the Babe. 'Doesn't want to run any risks.'

'Shouldn't wonder.'

'He's such a rotten head of the House, too,' said Vaughan. 'Ward may gas about my being headstrong and thoughtless, but I'm dashed if I would make a bally exhibition of myself like the Mutual.'

'What's he do?' enquired the Babe.

'It's not so much what he does. It's what he doesn't do that sickens me,' said Dallas. 'I may be a bit of a crock in some ways – for further details apply to Ward – but I can stop a couple of fags ragging if I try.'

'Can't Plunkett?'

'Not for nuts. He's simply helpless when there's anything going on that he ought to stop. Why, the other day there was a row in the fags' room that you could almost have heard at your place, Babe. We were up here working. The Mutual was jawing as usual on the subject of cramming tips for the Aeschylus exam. Said it wasn't scholarship, or some rot. What business is it of his how a chap works, I should like to know. Just as he had got under way, the fags began kicking up more row than ever.'

'I said', cut in Vaughan, 'that instead of minding other people's business, he'd better mind his own for a change, and go down and stop the row.'

'He looked a bit green at that,' said Dallas. 'Said the row didn't interfere with him. "Does with us," I said. "It's all very well for you. You aren't doing a stroke of work. No amount of row matters to a chap who's only delivering a rotten sermon on scholarship. Vaughan and I happen to be trying to do some work." "All right," he said, "if you want the row stopped, why don't you go and stop it? What's it got to do with me?"'

'Rotter!' interpolated the Babe.

'Wasn't he? Well, of course we couldn't stand that.'

'We crushed him,' said Vaughan.

'I said: "In my young days the head of the House used to keep order for himself." I asked him what he thought he was here for. Because he isn't ornamental. So he went down after that.'

'Well?' said the Babe. Being a miserable day boy he had had no experience of the inner life of a boarding House, which is the real life of a public school. His experience of life at St Austin's was limited to doing his work and playing centre-three-quarter for the fifteen. Which, it may be remarked in passing, he did extremely well.

Dallas took up the narrative. 'Well, after he'd been gone about five minutes, and the row seemed to be getting worse than ever, we thought we'd better go down and investigate. So we did.'

'And when we got to the fags' room,' said Vaughan, pointing the toasting-fork at the Babe by way of emphasis, 'there was the Mutual standing in the middle of the room gassing away with an expression on his face a cross between a village idiot and an unintelligent fried egg. And all round him was a seething mass of fags, half of them playing soccer with a top-hat and the other half cheering wildly whenever the Mutual opened his mouth.'

'What did you do?'

'We made an aggressive movement in force. Collared the hat, brained every fag within reach, and swore we'd report them to the beak and so on. They quieted down in about three and a quarter seconds by stopwatch, and we retired, taking the hat as a prize of war, and followed by the Mutual Friend.'

'He looked worried, rather,' said Vaughan. 'And, thank goodness, he let us alone for the rest of the evening.'

'That's only a sample, though,' explained Dallas. 'That sort of thing has been going on the whole term. If the head of a House is an abject lunatic, there's bound to be ructions. Fags simply live for the sake of kicking up rows. It's meat and drink to them.'

'I wish the Mutual would leave,' said Vaughan. 'Only that sort of chap always lingers on until he dies or gets sacked.'

'He's not the sort of fellow to get sacked, I should say,' said the Babe.

''Fraid not. I wish I could shunt into some other House. Between Ward and the Mutual life here isn't worth living.'

'There's Merevale's, now,' said Vaughan. 'I wish I was in there. In the first place you've got Merevale. He gets as near perfection as a beak ever does. Coaches the House footer and cricket, and takes an intelligent interest in things generally. Then there are some decent fellows in Merevale's. Charteris, Welch, Graham, Thomson, heaps of them.'

'Pity you came to Ward's,' said the Babe. 'Why did you?'

'My pater knew Ward a bit. If he'd known him well, he'd have sent me somewhere else.'

'My pater knew Vaughan's pater well, who knew Ward slightly and there you are. *Voilà comme des accidents arrivent.*'

'If Ward wanted to lug in a day boy to be head of the House,' said Vaughan, harping once more on the old string, 'he might at least have got somebody decent.'

'There's the great Babe himself. Babe, why don't you come in next term?'

'Not much,' said the Babe, with a shudder.

'Well, even barring present company, there are lots of chaps who would have jumped at the chance of being head of a House. But nothing would satisfy Ward but lugging the Mutual from the bosom of his beastly family.'

'We haven't decided that point about where he goes to,' said the Babe.

At this moment the door of the study opened, and the gentleman in question appeared in person. He stood in the doorway for a few seconds, gasping and throwing his arms about as if he found a difficulty in making his way in.

'I wish you two wouldn't make such an awful froust in the study *every* afternoon,' he observed, pleasantly. 'Have you been having a little tea-party? How nice!'

'We've been brewing, if that's what you mean,' said Vaughan, shortly.

'Oh,' said Plunkett, 'I hope you enjoyed yourselves. It's nearly lock-up, MacArthur.'

'That's Plunkett's delicate way of telling you you're not wanted, Babe.'

'Well, I suppose I ought to be going,' said the Babe. 'So long.'

And he went, feeling grateful to Providence for not having made his father, like the fathers of Vaughan and Dallas, a casual acquaintance of Mr Ward.

The Mutual Friend really was a trial to Vaughan and Dallas. Only those whose fate it is or has been to share a study with an uncongenial companion can appreciate their feelings to the full. Three in a study is always something of a tight fit, and when the three are in a state of perpetual warfare, or, at the best, of armed truce, things become very bad indeed.

'Do you find it necessary to have tea-parties every evening?' enquired Plunkett, after he had collected his books for the night's work. 'The smell of burnt meat—'

'Fried sausages,' said Vaughan. 'Perfectly healthy smell. Do you good.'

'It's quite disgusting. Really, the air in here is hardly fit to breathe.'

'You'll find an excellent brand of air down in the senior study,' said Dallas, pointedly. 'Don't stay and poison yourself here on *our* account,' he added. 'Think of your family.'

'I shall work where I choose,' said the Mutual Friend, with dignity.

'Of course, so long as you do work. You mustn't talk. Vaughan and I have got some Livy to do.'

Plunkett snorted, and the passage of arms ended, as it usually did, in his retiring with his books to the senior study, leaving Dallas and Vaughan to discuss his character once more in case there might be any points of it left upon which they had not touched in previous conversations.

'This robbery of the pots is a rum thing,' said Vaughan, thoughtfully, when the last shreds of Plunkett's character had been put through the mincing-machine to the satisfaction of all concerned.

'Yes. It's the sort of thing one doesn't think possible till it actually happens.'

'What the dickens made them put the things in the Pav. at all? They must have known it wouldn't be safe.'

'Well, you see, they usually cart them into the Board Room, I believe, only this time the governors were going to have a meeting there. They couldn't very well meet in a room with the table all covered with silver pots.'

'Don't see why.'

'Well, I suppose they could, really, but some of the governors are fairly nuts on strict form. There's that crock who makes the two-hour vote of thanks speeches on Prize Day. You can see him rising to a point of order, and fixing the Old 'Un with a fishy eye.'

'Well, anyhow, I don't see that they can blame a burglar for taking the pots if they simply chuck them in his way like that.'

'No. I say, we'd better weigh in with the Livy. The man Ward'll be round directly. Where's the dic? *And* our invaluable friend, Mr Bohn? Right. Now, you reel it off, and I'll keep an eye on the notes.' And they settled down to the business of the day.

After a while Vaughan looked up.

'Who's going to win the mile?' he asked.

'What's the matter with Thomson?'

'How about Drake then?'

'Thomson won the half.'

'I knew you'd say that. The half isn't a test of a chap's mile form. Besides, did you happen to see Drake's sprint?'

'Jolly good one.'

'I know, but look how late he started for it. Thomson crammed on the pace directly he got into the straight. Drake only began to put it on when he got to the Pav. Even then he wasn't far behind at the tape.'

'No. Well, I'm not plunging either way. Ought to be a good race.'

'Rather. I say, I wonder Welch doesn't try his hand at the mile. I believe he would do some rattling times if he'd only try.'

'Why, Welch is a sprinter.'

'I know. But I believe for all that that the mile's his distance. He's always well up in the cross-country runs.'

'Anyhow, he's not in for it this year. Thomson's my man. It'll be a near thing, though.'

'Jolly near thing. With Drake in front.'

'Thomson.'

'Drake.'

'All right, we'll see. Wonder why the beak doesn't come up. I can't sit here doing Livy all the evening. And yet if we stop he's bound to look in.'

'Oh Lord, is that what you've been worrying about? I thought you'd developed the work habit or something. Ward's all right. He's out on the tiles tonight. Gone to a dinner at Philpott's.'

'Good man, how do you know? Are you certain?'

'Heard him telling Prater this morning. Half the staff have gone. Good opportunity for a chap to go for a stroll if he wanted to. Shall we, by the way?'

'Not for me, thanks. I'm in the middle of a rather special book. Ever read *Great Expectations*? Dickens, you know.'

'I know. Haven't read it, though. Always rather funk starting on a classic, somehow. Good?'

'My dear chap! Good's not the word.'

'Well, after you. Exit Livy, then. And a good job, too. You might pass us the great Sherlock. Thanks.'

He plunged with the great detective into the mystery of the speckled band, while Vaughan opened *Great Expectations* at the place where he had left off the night before. And a silence fell upon the study.

Curiously enough, Dallas was not the only member of Ward's House to whom it occurred that evening that the absence of the House-master supplied a good opportunity for a stroll. The idea had also struck Plunkett favourably. He was not feeling very comfortable down-stairs. On entering the senior study he found Galloway, an Upper Fourth member of the House, already in possession. Galloway had managed that evening to insinuate himself with such success into the good graces of the matron, that he had been allowed to stay in the House instead of proceeding with the rest of the study to the Great Hall for preparation. The palpable failure of his attempt to hide the book he was reading under the table when he was disturbed led him to cast at the Mutual Friend, the cause of his panic, so severe and forbidding a look, that that gentleman retired, and made for the junior study.

The atmosphere in the junior study was close, and heavy with a blend of several strange odours. Plunkett went to the window. Then he noticed what he had never noticed before, that there were no bars to the window. Only the glass stood between him and the outer world. He threw up the sash as far as it would go. There was plenty of room to get out. So he got out. He stood for a moment inhaling the fresh air. Then, taking something from his coat-pocket, he dived into the shadows. An hour passed. In the study above, Dallas, surfeited with mysteries and villainy, put down his book and stretched himself.

'I say, Vaughan,' he said. 'Have you settled the House gym. team yet? It's about time the list went up.'

'Eh? What?' said Vaughan, coming slowly out of his book.

Dallas repeated his question.

'Yes,' said Vaughan, 'got it somewhere on me. Haynes, Jarvis, and myself are going in. Only, the Mutual has to stick up the list.'

It was the unwritten rule in Ward's, as in most of the other

Houses at the School, that none but the head of the House had the right of placing notices on the House board.

'I know,' said Dallas. 'I'll go and buck him up now.'

'Don't trouble. After prayers'll do.'

'It's all right. No trouble. Whom did you say? Yourself, Haynes—'

'And Jarvis. Not that he's any good. But the third string never matters much, and it'll do him good to represent the House.'

'Right. I'll go and unearth the Mutual.'

The result was that Galloway received another shock to his system.

'Don't glare, Galloway. It's rude,' said Dallas.

'Where's Plunkett got to?' he added.

'Junior study,' said Galloway.

Dallas went to the junior study. There were Plunkett's books on the table, but of their owner no signs were to be seen. The Mutual Friend had had the good sense to close the window after he had climbed through it, and Dallas did not suspect what had actually happened. He returned to Vaughan.

'The Mutual isn't in either of the studies,' he said. 'I didn't want to spend the evening playing hide-and-seek with him, so I've come back.'

'It doesn't matter, thanks all the same. Later on'll do just as well.'

'Do you object to the window going up?' asked Dallas. 'There's a bit of a froust on in here.'

'Rather not. Heave it up.'

Dallas hove it. He stood leaning out, looking towards the College buildings, which stood out black and clear against the April sky. From out of the darkness in the direction of Stapleton sounded the monotonous note of a corn-crake.

'Jove,' he said, 'it's a grand night. If I was at home now I shouldn't be cooped up indoors like this.'

'Holidays in another week,' said Vaughan, joining him. 'It is ripping, isn't it? There's something not half bad in the Coll. buildings on a night like this. I shall be jolly sorry to leave, in spite of Ward and the Mutual.'

'Same here, by Jove. We've each got a couple more years, though, if it comes to that. Hullo, prep.'s over.'

The sound of footsteps began to be heard from the direction of the College. Nine had struck from the School clock, and the Great Hall was emptying.

'Your turn to read at prayers, Vaughan. Hullo, there's the Mutual. Didn't hear him unlock the door. Glad he has, though. Saves us trouble.'

'I must be going down to look up a bit to read. Do you remember when Harper read the same bit six days running? I shall never forget Ward's pained expression. Harper explained that he thought the passage so beautiful that he couldn't leave it.'

'Why don't you try that tip?'

'Hardly. My reputation hasn't quite the stamina for the test.'

Vaughan left the room. At the foot of the stairs he was met by the matron.

'Will you unlock the door, please, Vaughan,' she said, handing him a bunch of keys. 'The boys will be coming in in a minute.'

'Unlock the door?' repeated Vaughan. 'I thought it was unlocked. All right.'

'By Jove,' he thought, 'the plot thickens. What is our only Plunkett doing out of the House when the door is locked, I wonder.'

Plunkett strolled in with the last batch of the returning crowd, wearing on his face the virtuous look of one who has been snatching a whiff of fresh air after a hard evening's preparation.

'Oh, I say, Plunkett,' said Vaughan, when they met in the study after prayers, 'I wanted to see you. Where have you been?'

'I have been in the junior study. Where did you think I had been?'

'Oh.'

'Do you doubt my word?'

'I've the most exaggerated respect for your word, but you weren't in the junior study at five to nine.'

'No, I went up to my dormitory about that time. You seem remarkably interested in my movements.'

'Only wanted to see you about the House gym. team. You might shove up the list tonight. Haynes, Jarvis, and myself.'

'Very well.'

'I didn't say anything to him,' said Vaughan to Dallas as they were going to their dormitories, 'but, you know, there's something jolly fishy about the Mutual. That door wasn't unlocked when we saw him outside. I unlocked it myself. Seems to me the Mutual's been having a little private bust of his own on the quiet.'

'That's rum. He might have been out by the front way to see one of the beaks, though.'

'Well, even then he would be breaking rules. You aren't allowed to go out after lock-up without House beak's leave. No, I find him guilty.'

'If only he'd go and get booked!' said Vaughan. 'Then he might have to leave. But he won't. No such luck.'

'No,' said Dallas. 'Good-night.'

'Good-night.'

Certainly there was something mysterious about the matter.

6 A LITERARY BANQUET

Charteris and Welch were conversing in the study of which they were the joint proprietors. That is to say, Charteris was talking and playing the banjo alternately, while Welch was deep in a book and refused to be drawn out of it under any pretext. Charteris' banjo was the joy of his fellows and the bane of his House-master. Being of a musical turn and owning a good deal of pocket-money, he had, at the end of the summer holidays, introduced the delights of a phonograph into the House. This being vetoed by the House-master, he had returned at the beginning of the following term with a penny whistle, which had suffered a similar fate. Upon this he had invested in a banjo, and the dazed Merevale, feeling that matters were getting beyond his grip, had effected a compromise with him. Having ascertained that there was no specific rule at St Austin's against the use of musical instruments, he had informed Charteris that if he saw fit to play the banjo before prep. only, and regarded the hours between seven and eleven as a close time, all should be forgiven, and he might play, if so disposed, till the crack of doom. To this reasonable request Charteris had promptly acceded, and peace had been restored. Charteris and Welch were a curious pair. Welch spoke very little. Charteris was seldom silent. They were both in the Sixth – Welch high up, Charteris rather low down.

In games, Welch was one of those fortunate individuals who are good at everything. He was captain of cricket, and not only captain, but also the best all-round man in the team, which is often a very different matter. He was the best wing three-quarter the School possessed; played fives and racquets like a professor, and only the day before had shared Tony's glory by winning the silver medal for fencing in the Aldershot competition.

The abilities of Charteris were more ordinary. He was a sound bat, and went in first for the Eleven, and played half for the Fifteen. As regards work, he might have been brilliant if he had chosen, but his energies were mainly devoted to the compilation of a monthly magazine (strictly unofficial) entitled *The Glow Worm*. This he edited, and for the most part wrote himself. It was a clever periodical, and rarely failed to bring him in at least ten shillings per number, after deducting the expenses which the College bookseller, who acted as sole agent, did his best to make as big as possible. Only a very few of the elect knew the identity of the editor, and they were bound to strict secrecy. On the day before the publication of each number, a notice was placed in the desk of the captain of each form, notifying him of what the morrow would bring forth, and asking him to pass it round the form. That was all. The School did the rest. *The Glow Worm* always sold well, principally because of the personal nature of its contents. If the average mortal is told that there is something about him in a paper, he will buy that paper at your own price.

Today he was giving his monthly tea in honour of the new number. Only contributors were invited, and the menu was always of the best. It was a *Punch* dinner, only more so, for these teas were celebrated with musical honours, and Charteris on the banjo was worth hearing. His rendering of extracts from the works of Messrs Gilbert and Sullivan was an intellectual treat.

'When I take the chair at our harmonic club!' he chanted, fixing the unconscious Welch with a fiery glance. 'Welch!'

'Yes.'

'If this is your idea of a harmonic club, it isn't mine. Put down that book, and try and be sociable.'

'One second,' said Welch, burrowing still deeper.

'That's what you always say,' said Charteris. 'Look here – Come in.'

There had been a knock at the door as he was speaking. Tony entered, accompanied by Jim. They were regular attendants at these banquets, for between them they wrote most of what was left of the magazine when Charteris had done with it. There was only one other contributor, Jackson, of Dawson's House, and he came in a few minutes later. Welch was the athletics expert of the paper, and did most of the match reports.

'Now we're complete,' said Charteris, as Jackson presented himself. 'Gentlemen – your seats. There are only four chairs, and we, as Wordsworth might have said, but didn't, are five. All right, I'll sit on the table. Welch, you worm, away with melancholy. Take away his book, somebody. That's right. Who says what? Tea already made. Coffee published shortly. If anybody wants cocoa, I've got some, only you'll have to boil more water. I regret the absence of menu-cards, but as the entire feast is visible to the naked eye, our loss is immaterial. The offertory will be for the Church expenses fund. Biscuits, please.'

'I wish you'd given this tea after next Saturday, Alderman,' said Jim. Charteris was called the Alderman on account of his figure, which was inclined to stoutness, and his general capacity for consuming food.

'Never put off till tomorrow – Why?'

'I simply must keep fit for the mile. How's Welch to run, too, if he eats this sort of thing?' He pointed to the well-spread board.

'Yes, there's something in that,' said Tony. 'Thank goodness, my little entertainment's over. I think I *will* try one of those chocolate things. Thanks.'

'Welch is all right,' said Jackson. 'He could win the hundred and the quarter on sausage-rolls. But think of the times.'

'And there,' observed Charteris, 'there, my young friend, you have touched upon a sore subject. Before you came in I was administering a few wholesome words of censure to that miserable object on your right. What is a fifth of a second more or less that it should make a man insult his digestion as Welch does? You'll hardly credit it, but for the last three weeks or more I have been forced to look on a fellow-being refusing pastry and drinking beastly extracts of meat, all for the sake of winning a couple of races. It quite put me off my feed. Cake, please. Good robust slice. Thanks.'

'It's rather funny when you come to think of it,' said Tony. 'Welch lives on Bovril for a month, and then, just as he thinks he's going to score, a burglar with a sense of humour strolls into the Pav., carefully selects the only two cups he had a chance of winning, and so to bed.'

'Leaving Master J. G. Welch an awful example of what comes of training,' said Jim. 'Welch, you're a rotter.'

'It isn't *my* fault,' observed Welch, plaintively. 'You chaps seem to think I've committed some sort of crime, just because a man I didn't know from Adam has bagged a cup or two.'

'It looks to me,' said Charteris, 'as if Welch, thinking his chances of the quarter rather rocky, hired one of his low acquaintances to steal the cup for him.'

'Shouldn't wonder. Welch knows some jolly low characters in Stapleton.'

'Welch is a jolly low character himself,' said Tony, judicially. 'I wonder you associate with him, Alderman.'

'Stand *in loco parentis*. Aunt of his asked me to keep an eye on him. "Dear George is so wild,"' she said.

Before Welch could find words to refute this hideous slander, Tony cut in once more.

'The only reason he doesn't drink gin and play billiards at the "Blue Lion" is that gin makes him ill and his best break at pills is six, including two flukes.'

'As a matter of fact,' said Welch, changing the conversation with a jerk, 'I don't much care if the cups are stolen. One doesn't only run for the sake of the pot.'

Charteris groaned. 'Oh, well,' said he, 'if you're going to take the high moral standpoint, and descend to brazen platitudes like that, I give you up.'

'It's a rum thing about those pots,' said Welch, meditatively.

'Seems to me,' Jim rejoined, 'the rum thing is that a man who considers the Pav. a safe place to keep a lot of valuable prizes in should be allowed at large. Why couldn't they keep them in the Board Room as they used to?'

'Thought it 'ud save trouble, I suppose. Save them carting the things over to the Pav. on Sports Day,' hazarded Tony.

'Saved the burglar a lot of trouble, I should say,' observed Jackson. 'I could break into the Pav. myself in five minutes.'

'Good old Jackson,' said Charteris, 'have a shot tonight. I'll hold the watch. I'm doing a leader on the melancholy incident for next month's *Glow Worm*. It appears that Master Reginald Robinson, a member of Mr Merevale's celebrated boarding-establishment, was passing by the Pavilion at an early hour on the morning of the second of April – that's today – when his eye was attracted by an excavation or incision in one of the windows of that imposing edifice. His narrative appears on another page. Interviewed by a *Glow Worm* representative, Master Robinson, who is a fine, healthy, bronzed young Englishman of some thirteen summers, with a delightful, boyish flow of speech, not wholly free from a suspicion of cheek, gave it as his opinion that the outrage was the work of a burglar – a remarkable display of sagacity in one so young. A portrait of Master Robinson appears on another page.'

'Everything seems to appear on another page,' said Jim. 'Am I to do the portrait?'

'I think it would be best. You can never trust a photo to caricature a person enough. Your facial H.B.'s the thing.'

'Have you heard whether anything else was bagged besides the cups?' asked Welch.

'Not that I know of,' said Jim.

'Yes there was,' said Jackson. 'It further appears that that lunatic, Adamson, had left some money in the pocket of his blazer, which he had left in the Pav. overnight. On enquiry it was found that the money had also left.'

Adamson was in the same House as Jackson, and had talked of nothing else throughout the whole of lunch. He was an abnormally wealthy individual, however, and it was generally felt, though he himself thought otherwise, that he could afford to lose some of the surplus.

'How much?' asked Jim.

'Two pounds.'

At this Jim gave vent to the exclamation which Mr Barry Pain calls the Englishman's shortest prayer.

'My dear sir,' said Charteris. 'My very dear sir. We blush for you. Might I ask *why* you take the matter to heart so?'

Jim hesitated.

'Better have it out, Jim,' said Tony. 'These chaps'll keep it dark all right.' And Jim entered once again upon the recital of his doings on the previous night.

'So you see,' he concluded, 'this two pound business makes it all the worse.'

'I don't see why,' said Welch.

'Well, you see, money's a thing everybody wants, whereas cups wouldn't be any good to a fellow at school. So that I should find it much harder to prove that I didn't take the two pounds, than I should have done to prove that I didn't take the cups.'

'But there's no earthly need for you to prove anything,' said Tony. 'There's not the slightest chance of your being found out.'

'Exactly,' observed Charteris. 'We will certainly respect your incog. if you wish it. Wild horses shall draw no evidence from us. It is, of course, very distressing, but what is man after all? Are we not as the beasts that perish, and is not our little life rounded by a sleep? Indeed, yes. And now – with full chorus, please.

'"We-e take him from the city or the plough.
We-e dress him up in uniform so ne-e-e-at."'

And at the third line some plaster came down from the ceiling, and Merevale came up, and the meeting dispersed without the customary cheers.

7 BARRETT EXPLORES

Barrett stood at the window of his study with his hands in his pockets, looking thoughtfully at the football field. Now and then he whistled. That was to show that he was very much at his ease. He whistled a popular melody of the day three times as slowly as its talented composer had originally intended it to be whistled, and in a strange minor key. Some people, when offended, invariably whistle in this manner, and these are just the people with whom, if you happen to share a study with them, it is rash to have differences of opinion. Reade, who was deep in a book – though not so deep as he would have liked the casual observer to fancy him to be – would have given much to stop Barrett's musical experiments. To ask him to stop in so many words was, of course, impossible. Offended dignity must draw the line somewhere. That is one of the curious results of a polite education. When two gentlemen of Hoxton or the Borough have a misunderstanding, they address one another with even more freedom than is their usual custom. When one member of a public school falls out with another member, his politeness in dealing with him becomes so Chesterfieldian, that one cannot help being afraid that he will sustain a strain from which he will never recover.

After a time the tension became too much for Barrett. He

picked up his cap and left the room. Reade continued to be absorbed in his book.

It was a splendid day outside, warm for April, and with just that freshness in the air which gets into the blood and makes Spring the best time of the whole year. Barrett had not the aesthetic soul to any appreciable extent, but he did know a fine day when he saw one, and even he realized that a day like this was not to be wasted in pottering about the School grounds watching the 'under thirteen' hundred yards (trial heats) and the 'under fourteen' broad jump, or doing occasional exercises in the gymnasium. It was a day for going far afield and not returning till lock-up. He had an object, too. Everything seemed to shout 'eggs' at him, to remind him that he was an enthusiast on the subject and had a collection to which he ought to seize this excellent opportunity of adding. The only question was, where to go. The surrounding country was a Paradise for the naturalist who had no absurd scruples on the subject of trespassing. To the west, in the direction of Stapleton, the woods and hedges were thick with nests. But then, so they were to the east along the Badgwick road. He wavered, but a recollection that there was water in the Badgwick direction, and that he might with luck beard a water-wagtail in its lair, decided him. What is life without a water-wagtail's egg? A mere mockery. He turned east.

'Hullo, Barrett, where are you off to?' Grey, of Prater's House, intercepted him as he was passing.

'Going to see if I can get some eggs. Are you coming?'

Grey hesitated. He was a keen naturalist, too.

'No, I don't think I will, thanks. Got an uncle coming down to see me.'

'Well, cut off before he comes.'

'No, he'd be too sick. Besides,' he added, ingenuously, 'there's a possible tip. Don't want to miss that. I'm simply stony. Always am at end of term.'

'Oh,' said Barrett, realizing that further argument would be thrown away. 'Well, so long, then.'

'So long. Hope you have luck.'

'Thanks. I say.'

'Well?'

'Roll-call, you know. If you don't see me anywhere about, you might answer my name.'

'All right. And if you find anything decent, you might remember me. You know pretty well what I've got already.'

'Right, I will.'

'Magpie's what I want particularly. Where are you going, by the way?'

'Thought of having a shot at old Venner's woods. I'm after a water-wagtail myself. Ought to be one or two in the Dingle.'

'Heaps, probably. But I should advise you to look out, you know. Venner's awfully down on trespassing.'

'Yes, the bounder. But I don't think he'll get me. One gets the knack of keeping fairly quiet with practice.'

'He's got thousands of keepers.'

'Millions.'

'Dogs, too.'

'Dash his beastly dogs. I like dogs. Why are you such a croaker today, Grey?'

'Well, you know he's had two chaps sacked for going in his woods to my certain knowledge, Morton-Smith and Ainsworth. That's only since I've been at the Coll., too. Probably lots more before that.'

'Ainsworth was booked smoking there. That's why he was

sacked. And Venner caught Morton-Smith himself simply staggering under dead rabbits. They sack any chap for poaching.'

'Well, I don't see how you're going to show you've not been poaching. Besides, it's miles out of bounds.'

'Grey,' said Barrett, severely, 'I'm surprised at you. Go away and meet your beastly uncle. Fancy talking about bounds at your time of life.'

'Well, don't forget me when you're hauling in the eggs.'

'Right you are. So long.'

Barrett proceeded on his way, his last difficulty safely removed. He could rely on Grey not to bungle that matter of roll-call. Grey had been there before.

A long white ribbon of dusty road separated St Austin's from the lodge gates of Badgwick Hall, the country seat of Sir Alfred Venner, M.P., also of 49A Lancaster Gate, London. Barrett walked rapidly for over half-an-hour before he came in sight of the great iron gates, flanked on the one side by a trim little lodge and green meadows, and on the other by woods of a darker green. Having got so far, he went on up the hill till at last he arrived at his destination. A small hedge, a sloping strip of green, and then the famous Dingle. I am loath to inflict any scenic rhapsodies on the reader, but really the Dingle deserves a line or two. It was the most beautiful spot in a country noted for its fine scenery. Dense woods were its chief feature. And by dense I mean well-supplied not only with trees (excellent things in themselves, but for the most part useless to the nest hunter), but also with a fascinating tangle of undergrowth, where every bush seemed to harbour eggs. All carefully preserved, too. That was the chief charm of the place. Since the sad episodes of Morton-Smith and Ainsworth, the School for the most part had looked askance at the Dingle. Once a select party from Dacre's House, headed by Babington, who always got himself into hot water when possible, had ventured into the forbidden land, and had returned hurriedly later in the afternoon with every sign of exhaustion, hinting breathlessly at keepers, dogs, and a pursuit that had lasted fifty minutes without a check. Since then no one had been daring enough to brave the terrors so carefully prepared for them by Milord Sir Venner and his minions, and the proud owner of the Dingle walked his woods in solitary state. Occasionally he would personally conduct some favoured guest thither and show him the wonders of the place. But this was not a frequent occurrence. On still-less frequent occasions, there were large shooting parties in the Dingle. But, as a rule, the word was 'Keepers only. No others need apply'.

A futile iron railing, some three feet in height, shut in the Dingle. Barrett jumped this lightly, and entered forthwith into Paradise. The place was full of nests. As Barrett took a step forward there was a sudden whirring of wings, and a bird rose from a bush close beside him. He went to inspect, and found a nest with seven eggs in it. Only a thrush, of course. As no one ever wants thrushes' eggs the world is over-stocked with them. Still, it gave promise of good things to come. Barrett pushed on through the bushes and the promise was fulfilled. He came upon another nest. Five eggs this time, of a variety he was unable with his moderate knowledge to classify. At any rate, he had not got them in his collection. Nor, to the best of his belief, had Grey. He took one for each of them.

Now this was all very well, thought Barrett, but what he had come for was the ovular deposit of the water-wagtail. Through the trees he could see the silver gleam of the brook at the foot of the hill. The woods sloped down to the very edge. Then came the brook, widening out here into the size of a small river. Then woods again all up the side of the opposite hill. Barrett hurried down the slope.

He had put on flannels for this emergency. He was prepared to wade, to swim if necessary. He hoped that it would not be necessary, for in April water is generally inclined to be chilly. Of keepers he had up till now seen no sign. Once he had heard the distant bark of a dog. It seemed to come from far across the stream and he had not troubled about it.

In the midst of the bushes on the bank stood a tree. It was not tall compared to the other trees of the Dingle, but standing alone as it did amongst the undergrowth it attracted the eye at once. Barrett, looking at it, saw something which made him forget water-wagtails for the moment. In a fork in one of the upper branches was a nest, an enormous nest, roughly constructed of sticks. It was a very jerry-built residence, evidently run up for the season by some prudent bird who knew by experience that no nest could last through the winter, and so had declined to waste his time in useless decorative work. But what bird was it? No doubt there are experts to whom a wood-pigeon's nest is something apart and distinct from the nest of the magpie, but to your unsophisticated amateur a nest that is large may be anything – rook's, magpie's, pigeon's, or great auk's. To such an one the only true test lies in the eggs. *Solvitur ambulando.* Barret laid the pill-boxes, containing the precious specimens he had found in the nest at the top of the hill, at the foot of the tree, and began to climb.

It was to be a day of surprises for him. When he had got half way up he found himself on a kind of ledge, which appeared to be a kind of junction at which the tree branched off into two parts. To the left was the nest, high up in its fork. To the right was another shoot. He realized at once, with keen disappointment, that it would be useless to go further. The branches were obviously not strong enough to bear his weight. He looked down, preparatory to commencing the descent, and to his astonishment found himself looking into a black cavern. In his eagerness to reach the nest he had not noticed before that the tree was hollow.

This made up for a great many things. His disappointment became less keen. Few things are more interesting than a hollow tree.

'Wonder how deep it goes down,' he said to himself. He broke off a piece of wood and dropped it down the hollow. It seemed to reach the ground uncommonly soon. He tried another piece. The sound of its fall came up to him almost simultaneously. Evidently the hole was not deep. He placed his hands on the edge, and let himself gently down into the darkness. His feet touched something solid almost immediately. As far as he could judge, the depth of the cavity was not more than five feet. Standing up at his full height he could just rest his chin on the edge.

He seemed to be standing on some sort of a floor, roughly made, but too regular to be the work of nature. Evidently someone had been here before. He bent down to make certain. There was more room to move about in than he suspected. A man sitting down would find it not uncomfortable.

He brushed his hand along the floor. Certainly it seemed to be constructed of boards. Then his hand hit something small and hard. He groped about until his fingers closed on it. It was – what was it? He could hardly make out for the moment. Suddenly, as he moved it, something inside it rattled. Now he knew what it was. It was the very thing he most needed, a box of matches.

The first match he struck promptly and naturally went out. No first match ever stays alight for more than three-fifths of a second. The second was more successful. The sudden light dazzled him for a moment. When his eyes had grown accustomed to it, the match went out. He lit a third, and this time he saw all round the little chamber.

'Great Scott,' he said, 'the place is a regular poultry shop.'

All round the sides were hung pheasants and partridges in various stages of maturity. Here and there the fur of a rabbit or a hare showed up amongst the feathers. Barrett hit on the solution of the problem directly. He had been shown a similar collection once in a tree on his father's land. The place was the headquarters of some poacher. Barrett was full of admiration for the ingenuity of the man in finding so safe a hiding-place.

He continued his search. In one angle of the tree was a piece of sacking. Barrett lifted it. He caught a glimpse of something bright, but before he could confirm the vague suspicion that flashed upon him, his match burnt down and lay smouldering on the floor. His hand trembled with excitement as he started to light another. It broke off in his hand. At last he succeeded. The light flashed up, and there beside the piece of sacking which had covered them were two cups. He recognized them instantly.

'Jove,' he gasped. 'The Sports pots! Now, how on earth—'

At this moment something happened which took his attention away from his discovery with painful suddenness. From beneath him came the muffled whine of a dog. He listened, holding his breath. No, he was not mistaken. The dog whined again, and broke into an excited bark. Somebody at the foot of the tree began to speak.

8 BARRETT CEASES TO EXPLORE

'Fetchimout!' said the voice, all in one word.

'Nice cheery remark to make!' thought Barrett. 'He'll have to do a good bit of digging before he fetches *me* out. I'm a fixture for the present.'

There was a sound of scratching as if the dog, in his eagerness to oblige, were trying to uproot the tree. Barrett, realizing that unless the keeper took it into his head to climb, which was unlikely, he was as safe as if he had been in his study at Philpott's, chuckled within himself, and listened intently.

'What is it, then?' said the keeper. 'Good dog, at 'em! Fetch him out, Jack.'

Jack barked excitedly, and redoubled his efforts.

The sound of scratching proceeded.

'R-r-r-ats–s-s!' said the mendacious keeper. Jack had evidently paused for breath. Barrett began quite to sympathize with him. The thought that the animal was getting farther away from the object of his search with every ounce of earth he removed, tickled him hugely. He would have liked to have been able to see the operations, though. At present it was like listening to a conversation through a telephone. He could only guess at what was going on.

Then he heard somebody whistling 'The Lincolnshire

Poacher', a strangely inappropriate air in the mouth of a keeper. The sound was too far away to be the work of Jack's owner, unless he had gone for a stroll since his last remark. No, it was another keeper. A new voice came up to him.

''Ullo, Ned, what's the dog after?'

'Thinks 'e's smelt a rabbit, seems to me.'

''Ain't a rabbit hole 'ere.'

'Thinks there is, anyhow. Look at the pore beast!'

They both laughed. Jack meanwhile, unaware that he was turning himself into an exhibition to make a keeper's holiday, dug assiduously. 'Come away, Jack,' said the first keeper at length. 'Ain't nothin' there. Ought to know that, clever dog like you.'

There was a sound as if he had pulled Jack bodily from his hole.

'Wait! 'Ere, Ned, what's that on the ground there?' Barrett gasped. His pill-boxes had been discovered. Surely they would put two and two together now, and climb the tree after him.

'Eggs. Two of 'em. 'Ow did they get 'ere, then?'

'It's one of them young devils from the School. Master says to me this morning, "Look out," 'e says, "Saunders, for them boys as come in 'ere after eggs, and frighten all the birds out of the dratted place. You keep your eyes open, Saunders," 'e says.'

'Well, if 'e's still in the woods, we'll 'ave 'im safe.'

'*If* he's still in the woods!' thought Barrett with a shiver.

After this there was silence. Barrett waited for what he thought was a quarter of an hour – it was really five minutes or less – then he peeped cautiously over the edge of his hiding-place. Yes, they had certainly gone, unless – horrible thought – they were waiting so close to the trunk of the tree as to be invisible from where he stood. He decided that the possibility must be risked. He was down on the ground in record time. Nothing happened. No hand shot out from its ambush to clutch him. He breathed more freely, and began to debate within himself which way to go. Up the hill it must be, of course, but should he go straight up, or to the left or to the right? He would have given much to know which way the keepers had gone, particularly he of the dog. They had separated, he knew. He began to reason the thing out. In the first place if they had separated, they must have gone different ways. It did not take him long to arrive at that conclusion. The odds, therefore, were that one had gone to the right up-stream, the other down-stream to the left. His knowledge of human nature told him that nobody would willingly walk up-hill if it was possible for him to walk on the flat. Therefore, assuming the two keepers to be human, they had gone along the valley. Therefore, his best plan would be to make straight for the top of the hill, as straight as he could steer, and risk it. Just as he was about to start, his eye caught the two pill-boxes, lying on the turf a few yards from where he had placed them.

'May as well take what I can get,' he thought. He placed them carefully in his pocket. As he did so a faint bark came to him on the breeze from down-stream. That must be friend Jack. He waited no longer, but dived into the bushes in the direction of the summit. He was congratulating himself on being out of danger – already he was more than half way up the hill – when suddenly he received a terrible shock. From the bushes to his left, not ten yards from where he stood, came the clear, sharp sound of a whistle. The sound was repeated, and this time an answer came from far out to his right. Before he could move another whistle joined in, again from the left, but farther off and higher up the hill than the first he had heard. He recalled what Grey had said about 'millions' of keepers. The expression, he thought, had understated the true facts, if anything. He remembered the case of Babington. It was a moment for action. No guile could save him now. It must be a stern chase for the rest of the distance. He drew a breath, and was off like an arrow. The noise he made was appalling. No one in the wood could help hearing it.

'Stop, there!' shouted someone. The voice came from behind, a fact which he noted almost automatically and rejoiced at. He had a start at any rate.

'Stop!' shouted the voice once again. The whistle blew like a steam siren, and once more the other two answered it. They were all behind him now. Surely a man of the public schools in flannels and gymnasium shoes, and trained to the last ounce for just such a sprint as this, could beat a handful of keepers in their leggings and heavy boots. Barrett raced on. Close behind him a crashing in the undergrowth and the sound of heavy breathing told him that keeper number one was doing his best. To left and right similar sounds were to be heard. But Barrett had placed these competitors out of the running at once. The race was between him and the man behind.

Fifty yards of difficult country, bushes which caught his clothes as if they were trying to stop him in the interests of law and order, branches which lashed him across the face, and rabbit-holes half hidden in the bracken, and still he kept his lead. He was increasing it. He must win now. The man behind was panting in deep gasps, for the pace had been warm and he was not in training. Barrett cast a glance over his shoulder, and as he looked the keeper's foot caught in a hole and he fell heavily. Barrett uttered a shout of triumph. Victory was his.

In front of him was a small hollow fringed with bushes. Collecting his strength he cleared these with a bound. Then another of the events of this eventful afternoon happened. Instead of the hard turf, his foot struck something soft, something which sat up suddenly with a yell. Barrett rolled down the slope and half-way up the other side like a shot rabbit. Dimly he recognized that he had jumped on to a human being. The figure did not wear the official velveteens. Therefore he had no business in the Dingle. And close behind thundered the keeper, now on his feet once more, dust on his clothes and wrath in his heart in equal proportions. 'Look out, man!' shouted Barrett, as the injured person rose to his feet. 'Run! Cut, quick! Keeper!' There was no time to say more. He ran. Another second and he was at the top, over the railing, and in the good, honest, public high-road again, safe. A hoarse shout of 'Got yer!' from below told a harrowing tale of capture. The stranger had fallen into the hands of the enemy. Very cautiously Barrett left the road and crept to the railing again. It was a rash thing to do, but curiosity overcame him. He had to see, or, if that was impossible, to hear what had happened.

For a moment the only sound to be heard was the gasping of the keeper. After a few seconds a rapidly nearing series of crashes announced the arrival of the man from the right flank of the pursuing forces, while almost simultaneously his colleague on the left came up.

Barrett could see nothing, but it was easy to understand what was going on. Keeper number one was exhibiting his prisoner. His narrative, punctuated with gasps, was told mostly in hoarse whispers, and Barrett missed most of it.

'Foot (gasp) rabbit-'ole.' More gasps. 'Up agen . . . minute . . . (indistinct mutterings) . . . and (triumphantly) COTCHED 'IM!'

Exclamations of approval from the other two. 'I assure you,' said another voice. The prisoner was having his say. 'I assure you that I was doing no harm whatever in this wood. I . . .'

'Better tell that tale to Sir Alfred,' cut in one of his captors.

‘’E’ll learn yer,’ said the keeper previously referred to as number one, vindictively. He was feeling shaken up with his run and his heavy fall, and his temper was proportionately short.

‘I swear I’ve heard that voice before somewhere,’ thought Barrett. ‘Wonder if it’s a Coll. chap.’

Keeper number one added something here, which was inaudible to Barrett.

‘I tell you I’m not a poacher,’ said the prisoner, indignantly. ‘And I object to your language. I tell you I was lying here doing nothing and some fool or other came and jumped on me. I . . .’

The rest was inaudible. But Barrett had heard enough.

‘I knew I’d heard that voice before. Plunkett, by Jove! Golly, what *is* the world coming to, when heads of Houses and School-prefects go on the poach! Fancy! Plunkett of all people, too! This is a knock-out, I’m hanged if it isn’t.’

From below came the sound of movement. The keepers were going down the hill again. To Barrett’s guilty conscience it seemed that they were coming up. He turned and fled.

The hedge separating Sir Alfred Venner’s land from the road was not a high one, though the drop the other side was considerable. Barrett had not reckoned on this. He leapt the hedge, and staggered across the road. At the same moment a grey-clad cyclist, who was pedalling in a leisurely manner in the direction of the School, arrived at the spot. A collision seemed imminent, but the stranger in a perfectly composed manner, as if he had suddenly made up his mind to take a sharp turning, rode his machine up the bank, whence he fell with easy grace to the road, just in time to act as a cushion for Barrett. The two lay there in a tangled heap. Barrett was the first to rise.

9 ENTER THE SLEUTH-HOUND

'I'm awfully sorry,' he said, disentangling himself carefully from the heap. 'I hope you're not hurt.'

The man did not reply for a moment. He appeared to be laying the question before himself as an impartial judge, as who should say: 'Now tell me candidly, *are* you hurt? Speak freely and without bias.'

'No,' he said at last, feeling his left leg as if he were not absolutely easy in his mind about that, 'no, not hurt, thank you. Not much, that is,' he added with the air of one who thinks it best to qualify too positive a statement. 'Left leg. Shin. Slight bruise. Nothing to signify.'

'It was a rotten thing to do, jumping over into the road like that,' said Barrett. 'Didn't remember there'd be such a big drop.'

'My fault in a way,' said the man. 'Riding wrong side of road. Out for a run?'

'More or less.'

'Excellent thing.'

'Yes.'

It occurred to Barrett that it was only due to the man on whom he had been rolling to tell him the true facts of the case. Besides, it might do something towards removing the impression which must, he felt, be forming in the stranger's mind that he was mad.

'You see,' he said, in a burst of confidence, 'it was rather a close thing. There were some keepers after me.'

'Ah!' said the man. 'Thought so. Trespassing?'

'Yes.'

'Ah. Keepers don't like trespassers. Curious thing – don't know if it ever occurred to you – if there were no trespassers, there would be no need for keepers. To their interest, then, to encourage trespassers. But do they?'

Barrett admitted that they did not very conspicuously.

'No. Same with all professions. Not poaching, I suppose?'

'Rather not. I was after eggs. By Jove, that reminds me.' He felt in his pocket for the pill-boxes. Could they have survived the stormy times through which they had been passing? He heaved a sigh of relief as he saw that the eggs were uninjured. He was so intent on examining them that he missed the stranger's next remark.

'Sorry. What? I didn't hear.'

'Asked if I was going right for St Austin's School.'

'College!' said Barrett with a convulsive shudder. The most deadly error mortal man can make, with the exception of calling a school a college, is to call a college a school.

'College!' said the man. 'Is this the road?'

'Yes. You can't miss it. I'm going there myself. It's only about a mile.'

'Ah,' said the man, with a touch of satisfaction in his voice. 'Going there yourself, are you? Perhaps you're one of the scholars?'

'Not much,' said Barrett, 'ask our form-beak if I'm a scholar. Oh. I see. Yes, I'm there all right.'

Barrett was a little puzzled as to how to class his companion. No old public school man would talk of scholars. And yet he was emphatically not a bargee. Barrett set him down as a sort of superior tourist, a Henry as opposed to an 'Arry.

'Been bit of a disturbance there, hasn't there? Cricket pavilion. Cups.'

'Rather. But how on earth—'

'How on earth did I get to hear of it, you were going to say. Well, no need to conceal anything. Fact is, down here to look into the matter. Detective. Name, Roberts, Scotland Yard. Now we know each other, and if you can tell me one or two things about this burglary, it would be a great help to me, and I should be very much obliged.'

Barrett had heard that a detective was coming down to look into the affair of the cups. His position was rather a difficult one. In a sense it was simple enough. He had found the cups. He could (keepers permitting) go and fetch them now, and there would – No. There would *not* be an end of the matter. It would be very pleasant, exceedingly pleasant, to go to the Headmaster and the detective, and present the cups to them with a 'Bless you, my children' air. The Headmaster would say, 'Barrett, you're a marvel. How can I thank you sufficiently?' while the detective would observe that he had been in the profession over twenty years, but never had he seen so remarkable an exhibition of sagacity and acumen as this. That, at least, was what ought to take place. But Barrett's experience of life, short as it was, had taught him the difference between the ideal and the real. The real, he suspected, would in this case be painful. Certain facts would come to light. When had he found the cups? About four in the afternoon? Oh. Roll-call took place at four in the afternoon. How came it that he was not at roll-call? Furthermore, how came it that he was marked on the list as having answered his name at that ceremony? Where had he found the cups? In a hollow tree?

Just so. Where was the hollow tree? In Sir Alfred Venner's woods. Did he know that Sir Alfred Venner's woods were out of bounds? Did he know that, in consequence of complaints from Sir Alfred Venner, Sir Alfred Venner's woods were more out of bounds than any other out of bounds woods in the entire county that did *not* belong to Sir Alfred Venner? He did? Ah! No, the word for his guidance in this emergency, he felt instinctively, was 'mum'. Time might provide him with a solution. He might, for instance, abstract the cups secretly from their resting-place, place them in the middle of the football field, and find them there dramatically after morning school. Or he might reveal his secret from the carriage window as his train moved out of the station on the first day of the holidays. There was certain to be some way out of the difficulty. But for the present, silence.

He answered his companion's questions freely, however. Of the actual burglary he knew no more than any other member of the School, considerably less, indeed, than Jim Thomson, of Merevale's, at present staggering under the weight of a secret even more gigantic than Barrett's own. In return for his information he extracted sundry reminiscences. The scar on the detective's cheekbone, barely visible now, was the mark of a bullet, which a certain burglar, named, singularly enough, Roberts, had fired at him from a distance of five yards. The gentleman in question, who, the detective hastened to inform Barrett, was no relation of his, though owning the same name, happened to be a poor marksman and only scored a bad outer, assuming the detective's face to have been the bull. He also turned up his cuff to show a larger scar. This was another testimonial from the burglar world. A Kensington practitioner had had the bad taste to bite off a piece of that part of the detective. In short, Barrett enlarged his knowledge of the seamy side of things considerably in the mile of road which had to be traversed before St Austin's appeared in sight. The two parted at the big gates, Barrett going in the direction of Philpott's, the detective wheeling his machine towards the porter's lodge.

Barrett's condition when he turned in at Philpott's door was critical. He was so inflated with news that any attempt to keep it in might have serious results. Certainly he could not sleep that night in such a bomb-like state.

It was thus that he broke in upon Reade. Reade had passed an absurdly useless afternoon. He had not stirred from the study. For all that it would have mattered to him, it might have been raining hard the whole afternoon, instead of being, as it had been, the finest afternoon of the whole term. In a word, and not to put too fine a point on the matter, he had been frousting, and consequently was feeling dull and sleepy, and generally under-vitalized and futile. Barrett entered the study with a rush, and was carried away by excitement to such an extent that he addressed Reade as if the deadly feud between them not only did not exist, but never had existed.

'I say, Reade. Heave that beastly book away. My aunt, I have had an afternoon of it.'

'Oh?' said Reade, politely, 'where did you go?'

'After eggs in the Dingle.'

Reade was fairly startled out of his dignified reserve. For the first time since they had had their little difference, he addressed Barrett in a sensible manner.

'You idiot!' he said.

'Don't see it. The Dingle's just the place to spend a happy day. Like Rosherville. Jove, it's worth going there. You should see the birds. Place is black with 'em.'

'How about keepers? See any?'

'Did I not! Three of them chased me like good 'uns all over the place.'

'You got away all right, though.'

'Only just. I say, do you know what happened? You know that rotter Plunkett. Used to be a day boy. Head of Ward's now. Wears specs.'

'Yes?'

'Well, just as I was almost out of the wood, I jumped a bush and landed right on top of him. The man was asleep or something. Fancy choosing the Dingle of all places to sleep in, where you can't go a couple of yards without running into a keeper! He hadn't even the sense to run. I yelled to him to look out, and then I hooked it myself. And then the nearest keeper, who'd just come down a buster over a rabbit-hole, sailed in and had him. I couldn't do anything, of course.'

'Jove, there'll be a fair-sized row about this. The Old Man's on to trespassing like tar. I say, think Plunkett'll say anything about you being there too?'

'Shouldn't think so. For one thing I don't think he recognized me. Probably doesn't know me by sight, and he was fast asleep, too. No, I fancy I'm all right.'

'Well, it was a jolly narrow shave. Anything else happen?'

'Anything else! Just a bit. That's to say, no, nothing much else. No.'

'Now then,' said Reade, briskly. 'None of your beastly mysteries. Out with it.'

'Look here, swear you'll keep it dark?'

'Of course I will.'

'On your word of honour?'

'If you think—' began Reade in an offended voice.

'No, it's all right. Don't get shirty. The thing is, though, it's so frightfully important to keep it dark.'

'Well? Buck up.'

'Well, you needn't believe me, of course, but I've found the pots.'

Reade gasped.

'What!' he cried. 'The pot for the quarter?'

'And the one for the hundred yards. Both of them. It's a fact.'

'But where? How? What have you done with them?'

Barrett unfolded his tale concisely.

'You see,' he concluded, 'what a hole I'm in. I can't tell the Old Man anything about it, or I get booked for cutting roll-call, and going out of bounds. And then, while I'm waiting and wondering what to do, and all that, the thief, whoever he is, will most likely go off with the pots. What do you think I ought to do?'

Reade perpended.

'Well,' he said, 'all you can do is to lie low and trust to luck, as far as I can see. Besides, there's one consolation. This Plunkett business'll make every keeper in the Dingle twice as keen after trespassers. So the pot man won't get a chance of getting the things away.'

'Yes, there's something in that,' admitted Barrett.

'It's all you can do,' said Reade.

'Yes. Unless I wrote an anonymous letter to the Old Man explaining things. How would that do?'

'Do for you, probably. Anonymous letters always get traced to the person who wrote them. Or pretty nearly always. No, you simply lie low.'

'Right,' said Barrett, 'I will.'

The process of concealing one's superior knowledge is very

irritating. So irritating, indeed, that very few people do it. Barrett, however, was obliged to by necessity. He had a good chance of displaying his abilities in that direction when he met Grey the next morning.

'Hullo,' said Grey, 'have a good time yesterday?'

'Not bad. I've got an egg for you.'

'Good man. What sort?'

'Hanged if I know. I know you haven't got it, though.'

'Thanks awfully. See anything of the million keepers?'

'Heard them oftener than I saw them.'

'They didn't book you?'

'Rather fancy one of them saw me, but I got away all right.'

'Find the place pretty lively?'

'Pretty fair.'

'Stay there long?'

'Not very.'

'No. Thought you wouldn't. What do you say to a small ice? There's time before school.'

'Thanks. Are you flush?'

'Flush isn't the word for it. I'm a plutocrat.'

'Uncle came out fairly strong then?'

'Rather. To the tune of one sovereign, cash. He's a jolly good sort, my uncle.'

'So it seems,' said Barrett.

The meeting then adjourned to the School shop, Barrett enjoying his ice all the more for the thought that his secret still was a secret. A thing which it would in all probability have ceased to be, had he been rash enough to confide it to K. St H. Grey, who, whatever his other merits, was very far from being the safest sort of confidant. His usual practice was to speak first, and to think, if at all, afterwards.

10 MR THOMPSON INVESTIGATES

The Pavilion burglary was discussed in other places besides Charteris' study. In the Masters' Common Room the matter came in for its full share of comment. The masters were, as at most schools, divided into the athletic and non-athletic, and it was for the former class that the matter possessed most interest. If it had been that apple of the College Library's eye, the original MS. of St Austin's private diary, or even that lesser treasure, the black-letter Eucalyptides, that had disappeared, the elder portion of the staff would have had a great deal to say upon the subject. But, apart from the excitement caused by the strangeness of such an occurrence, the theft of a couple of Sports prizes had little interest for them.

On the border-line between these two castes came Mr Thompson, the Master of the Sixth Form, spelt with a *p* and no relation to the genial James or the amiable Allen, with the former of whom, indeed, he was on very indifferent terms of friendship. Mr Thompson, though an excellent classic, had no knowledge of the inwardness of the Human Boy. He expected every member of his form not only to be earnest – which very few members of a Sixth Form are – but also to communicate his innermost thoughts to him. His aim was to be their confidant, the wise friend to whom they were to bring their troubles and come for advice. He was, in fact, poor man, the good young master. Now, it is generally the case at school that troubles are things to be worried through alone, and any attempt at interference is usually resented. Mr Thompson had asked Jim to tea, and, while in the very act of passing him the muffins, had embarked on a sort of unofficial sermon, winding up by inviting confidences. Jim had naturally been first flippant, and then rude, and relations had been strained ever since.

'It must have been a professional,' alleged Perkins, the master of the Upper Fourth. 'If it hadn't been for the fact of the money having been stolen as well as the cups, I should have put it down to one of our fellows.'

'My dear Perkins,' expostulated Merevale.

'My dear Merevale, my entire form is capable of any crime except the theft of money. A boy might have taken the cups for a joke, or just for the excitement of the thing, meaning to return them in time for the Sports. But the two pounds knocks that on the head. It must have been a professional.'

'I always said that the Pavilion was a very unsafe place in which to keep anything of value,' said Mr Thompson.

'You were profoundly right, Thompson,' replied Perkins. 'You deserve a diploma.'

'This business is rather in your line, Thompson,' said Merevale. 'You must bring your powers to bear on the subject, and scent out the criminal.'

Mr Thompson took a keen pride in his powers of observation. He would frequently observe, like the lamented Sherlock Holmes, the vital necessity of taking notice of trifles. The daily life of a Sixth Form master at a big public school does not afford much scope for the practice of the detective art, but Mr Thompson had once detected a piece of cribbing, when correcting some Latin proses for the master of the Lower Third, solely by the exercise of his powers of observation, and he had never forgotten it. He burned to add another scalp to his collection, and this Pavilion burglary seemed peculiarly suited to his talents. He had given the matter his attention, and, as far as he could see, everything pointed to the fact that skilled hands had been at work.

From eleven until half-past twelve that day, the Sixth were doing an unseen examination under the eye of the Headmaster, and Mr Thompson was consequently off duty. He took advantage of this to stroll down to the Pavilion and make a personal inspection of the first room, from which what were left of the prizes had long been removed to a place of safety.

He was making his way to the place where the ground-man was usually to be found, with a view to obtaining the keys, when he noticed that the door was already open, and on going thither he came upon Biffen, the ground-man, in earnest conversation with a stranger.

'Morning, sir,' said the ground-man. He was on speaking terms with most of the masters and all the boys. Then, to his companion, 'This is Mr Thompson, one of our masters.'

'Morning, sir,' said the latter. 'Weather keeps up. I am Inspector Roberts, Scotland Yard. But I think we're in for rain soon. Yes. 'Fraid so. Been asked to look into this business, Mr Thompson. Queer business.'

'Very. Might I ask – I am very interested in this kind of thing – whether you have arrived at any conclusions yet?'

The detective eyed him thoughtfully, as if he were hunting for the answer to a riddle.

'No. Not yet. Nothing definite.'

'I presume you take it for granted it was the work of a professional burglar.'

'No. No. Take nothing for granted. Great mistake. Prejudices one way or other great mistake. But, I think, yes, I think it was probably almost certainly – *not* done by a professional.'

Mr Thompson looked rather blank at this. It shook his confidence in his powers of deduction.

'But,' he expostulated. 'Surely no one but a practised burglar would have taken a pane of glass out so – ah – neatly?'

Inspector Roberts rubbed a finger thoughtfully round the place where the glass had been. Then he withdrew it, and showed a small cut from which the blood was beginning to drip.

'Do you notice anything peculiar about that cut?' he enquired.

Mr Thompson did not. Nor did the ground-man.

'Look carefully. Now do you see? No? Well, it's not a clean cut. Ragged. Very ragged. Now if a professional had cut that pane out he wouldn't have left it jagged like that. No. He would have used a diamond. Done the job neatly.'

This destroyed another of Mr Thompson's premises. He had taken it for granted that a diamond had been used.

'Oh!' he said, 'was that pane not cut by a diamond; what did the burglar use, then?'

'No. No diamond. Diamond would have left smooth surface. Smooth as a razor edge. This is like a saw. Amateurish work. Can't say for certain, but probably done with a chisel.'

'With a chisel? Surely not.'

'Yes. Probably with a chisel. Probably the man knocked the pane out with one blow, then removed all the glass so as to make it look like the work of an old hand. Very good idea, but amateurish. I am told that three cups have been taken. Could you tell me how long they had been in the Pavilion?'

Mr Thompson considered.

'Well,' he said. 'Of course it's difficult to remember exactly, but I think they were placed there soon after one o'clock the day before yesterday.'

'Ah! And the robbery took place yesterday in the early morning, or the night before?'

'Yes.'

'Is the Pavilion the usual place to keep the prizes for the Sports?'

'No, it is not. They were only put there temporarily. The Board Room, where they are usually kept, and which is in the main buildings of the School, happened to be needed until the next day. Most of us were very much against leaving them in the Pavilion, but it was thought that no harm could come to them if they were removed next day.'

'But they were removed that night, which made a great difference,' said Mr Roberts, chuckling at his mild joke. 'I see. Then I suppose none outside the School knew that they were not in their proper place?'

'I imagine not.'

'Just so. Knocks the idea of professional work on the head. None of the regular trade can have known this room held so much silver for one night. No regular would look twice at a cricket pavilion under ordinary circumstances. Therefore, it must have been somebody who had something to do with the School. One of the boys, perhaps.'

'Really, I do not think that probable.'

'You can't tell. Never does to form hasty conclusions. Boy might have done it for many reasons. Some boys would have done it for the sake of the excitement. That, perhaps, is the least possible explanation. But you get boy kleptomaniacs just as much in proportion as grown-up kleptomaniacs. I knew a man. Had a son. Couldn't keep him away from anything valuable. Had to take him away in a hurry from three schools, good schools, too.'

'Really? What became of him? He did not come to us, I suppose?'

'No. Somebody advised the father to send him to one of those North-Country schools where they flog. Great success. Stole some money. Got flogged, instead of expelled. Did it again with same result. Gradually got tired of it. Reformed character now . . . I don't say it is a boy, mind you. Most probably not. Only say it may be.'

All the while he was talking, his eyes were moving restlessly round the room. He came to the window through which Jim had effected his entrance, and paused before the broken pane.

'I suppose he tried that window first, before going round to the other?' hazarded Mr Thompson.

'Yes. Most probably. Broke it, and then remembered that anyone at the windows of the boarding Houses might see him, so left his job half done, and shifted his point of action. I think so. Yes.'

He moved on again till he came to the other window. Then he gave vent to an excited exclamation, and picked up a piece of caked mud from the sill as carefully as if it were some fragile treasure.

'Now, see this,' he said. 'This was wet when the robbery was done. The man brought it in with him. On his boot. Left it on the sill as he climbed in. Got out in a hurry, startled by something – you can see he was startled and left in a hurry from the different values of the cups he took – and as he was going, put his hand on this. Left a clear impression. Good as plaster of Paris very nearly.'

Mr Thompson looked at the piece of mud, and there, sure enough, was the distinct imprint of the palm of a hand. He could see the larger of the lines quite clearly, and under a magnifying-glass there was no doubt that more could be revealed.

He drew in a long breath of satisfaction and excitement.

'Yes,' said the detective. 'That piece of mud couldn't prove anything by itself, but bring it up at the end of a long string of evidence, and if it fits your man, it convicts him as much as a snap-shot photograph would. Morning, sir. I must be going.' And he retired, carrying the piece of mud in his hand, leaving Mr Thompson in the full grip of the detective-fever, hunting with might and main for more clues.

After some time, however, he was reluctantly compelled to give up the search, for the bell rang for dinner, and he always lunched, as did many of the masters, in the Great Hall. During the course of the meal he exercised his brains without pause in the effort to discover a fitting suspect. Did he know of any victim of kleptomania in the School? No, he was sorry to say he did not. Was anybody in urgent need of money? He could not say. Very probably yes, but he had no means of knowing.

After lunch he went back to the Common Room. There was a letter lying on the table. He picked it up. It was addressed to 'J. Thomson, St Austin's'. Now Mr Thompson's Christian name was John. He did not notice the omission of the *p* until he had opened the envelope and caught a glimpse of the contents. The letter was so short that only a glimpse was needed, and it was not till he had read the whole that he realized that it was somebody else's letter that he had opened.

This was the letter:

'Dear Jim – Frantic haste. Can you let me have that two pounds directly you come back? Beg, borrow, or steal it. I simply must have it. – Yours ever,

Allen.'

11 THE SPORTS

Sports weather at St Austin's was as a rule a quaint but unpleasant solution of mud, hail, and iced rain. These were taken as a matter of course, and the School counted it as something gained when they were spared the usual cutting east wind.

This year, however, occurred that invaluable exception which is so useful in proving rules. There was no gale, only a gentle breeze. The sun was positively shining, and there was a general freshness in the air which would have made a cripple cast away his crutches, and, after backing himself heavily both ways, enter for the Strangers' Hundred Yards.

Jim had wandered off alone. He was feeling too nervous at the thought of the coming mile and all it meant to him to move in society for the present. Charteris, Welch, and Tony, going out shortly before lunch to inspect the track, found him already on the spot, and in a very low state of mind.

'Hullo, you chaps,' he said dejectedly, as they came up.

'Hullo.'

'Our James is preoccupied,' said Charteris. 'Why this jaundiced air, Jim? Look at our other Thompson over there.'

'Our other Thompson' was at that moment engaged in conversation with the Headmaster at the opposite side of the field.

'Look at him,' said Charteris, 'prattling away as merrily as a little che-ild to the Old Man. You should take a lesson from him.'

'Look here, I say,' said Jim, after a pause, 'I believe there's something jolly queer up between Thompson and the Old Man, and I believe it's about me.'

'What on earth makes you think that?' asked Welch.

'It's his evil conscience,' said Charteris. 'No one who hadn't committed the awful crime that Jim has, could pay the least attention to anything Thompson said. What does our friend Thucydides remark on the subject? –

> '"*Conscia mens recti, nec si sinit esse dolorem*
> *Sed revocare gradum.*"

Very well then.'

'But why should you think anything's up?' asked Tony.

'Perhaps nothing is, but it's jolly fishy. You see Thompson and the Old 'Un pacing along there? Well, they've been going like that for about twenty minutes. I've been watching them.'

'But you can't tell they're talking about you, you rotter,' said Tony. 'For all you know they may be discussing the exams.'

'Or why the sea is boiling hot, and whether pigs have wings,' put in Charteris.

'Or anything,' added Welch profoundly.

'Well, all I know is that Thompson's been doing all the talking, and the Old Man's been getting more and more riled.'

'Probably Thompson's been demanding a rise of screw or asking for a small loan or something,' said Charteris. 'How long have you been watching them?'

'About twenty minutes.'

'From here?'

'Yes.'

'Why didn't you go and join them? There's nothing like tact. If you were to go and ask the Old Man why the whale wailed or something after that style it 'ud buck him up like a tonic. I wish you would. And then you could tell him to tell you all about it and see if you couldn't do something to smooth the wrinkles from his careworn brow and let the sunshine of happiness into his heart. He'd like it awfully.'

'Would he!' said Jim grimly. 'Well, I got the chance just now. Thompson said something to him, and he spun round, saw me, and shouted "Thomson". I went up and capped him, and he was starting to say something when he seemed to change his mind, and instead of confessing everything, he took me by the arm, and said, "No, no, Thomson. Go away. It's nothing. I will send for you later."'

'And did you knock him down?' asked Charteris.

'What happened?' said Welch.

'He gave me a shove as if he were putting the weight, and said again, "It's no matter. Go away, Thomson, now." So I went.'

'And you've kept an eye on him ever since?' said Charteris. 'Didn't he seem at all restive?'

'I don't think he noticed me. Thompson had the floor and he was pretty well full up listening to him.'

'I suppose you don't know what it's all about?' asked Tony.

'Must be this Pavilion business.'

'Now, my dear, sweet cherub,' said Charteris, 'don't you go and make an utter idiot of yourself and think you're found out and all that sort of thing. Even if they suspect you they've got to prove it. There's no sense in your giving them a helping hand in the business. What you've got to do is to look normal. Don't overdo it or you'll look like a swashbuckler, and that'll be worse than underdoing it. Can't you make yourself look less like a convicted forger? For my sake?'

'You really do look a bit off it,' said Welch critically. 'As if you were sickening for the flu., or something. Doesn't he, Tony?'

'Rather!' said that expert in symptoms. 'You simply must buck up, Jim, or Drake'll walk away from you.'

'It's disappointing,' said Charteris, 'to find a chap who can crack a crib as neatly as you can doubling up like this. Think how Charles Peace would have behaved under the circs. Don't disgrace him, poor man.'

'Besides,' said Jim, with an attempt at optimism, 'it isn't as if I'd actually done anything, is it?'

'Just so,' said Charteris, 'that's what I've been trying to get you to see all along. Keep that fact steadily before you, and you'll be all right.'

'There goes the lunch-bell,' said Tony. 'You can always tell Merevale's bell in a crowd. William rings it as if he was doing it for his health.'

William, also known in criminal circles as the Moke, was the gentleman who served the House – in a perpetual grin and a suit of livery four sizes too large for him – as a sort of butler.

'He's an artist,' agreed Charteris, as he listened to the performance. 'Does it as if he enjoyed it, doesn't he? Well, if we don't want to spoil Merevale's appetite by coming in at half-time, we might be moving.' They moved accordingly.

The Sports were to begin at two o'clock with a series of hundred-yards races, which commenced with the 'under twelve' (Cameron of Prater's a warm man for this, said those who had means of knowing), and culminated at about a quarter past with the open event, for which Welch was a certainty. By a quarter to the hour the places round the ropes were filled, and more visitors were constantly streaming in at the two entrances to the School grounds, while in the centre of the ring the band of the local police force – the military being unavailable owing to exigencies of distance – were seating themselves with the grim determination of those who know that they are going to play the soldiers' chorus out of *Faust*. The band at the Sports had played the soldiers' chorus out of *Faust* every year for decades past, and will in all probability play it for decades to come.

The Sports at St Austin's were always looked forward to by everyone with the keenest interest, and when the day arrived, were as regularly voted slow. In all school sports there are too many foregone conclusions. In the present instance everybody knew, and none better than the competitors themselves, that Welch would win the quarter and hundred. The high jump was an equal certainty for a boy named Reece in Halliday's House. Jackson, unless he were quite out of form, would win the long jump, and the majority of the other events had already been decided. The gem of the afternoon would be the mile, for not even the shrewdest judge of form could say whether Jim would beat Drake, or Drake Jim. Both had done equally good times in practice, and both were known to be in the best of training. The adherents of Jim pointed to the fact that he had won the half off Drake – by a narrow margin, true, but still he had won it. The other side argued that a half-mile is no criterion for a mile, and that if Drake had timed his sprint better he would probably have won, for he had finished up far more strongly than his opponent. And so on the subject of the mile, public opinion was for once divided.

The field was nearly full by this time. The only clear space outside the ropes was where the Headmaster stood to greet and talk about the weather to such parents and guardians and other celebrities as might pass. This habit of his did not greatly affect the unattached members of the School, those whose parents lived in distant parts of the world and were not present on Sports Day, but to St Jones Brown (for instance) of the Lower Third, towing Mr Brown, senior, round the ring, it was a nervous ordeal to have to stand by while his father and the Head exchanged polite commonplaces. He could not help feeling that there was *just a chance* (horrible thought) that the Head, searching for something to say, might seize upon that little matter of broken bounds or shaky examination papers as a subject for discussion. He was generally obliged, when the interview was over, to conduct his parent to the shop by way of pulling his system together again, the latter, of course, paying.

At intervals round the ropes Old Austinian number one was meeting Old Austinian number two (whom he emphatically detested, and had hoped to avoid), and was conversing with him in a nervous manner, the clearness of his replies being greatly handicapped by a feeling, which grew with the minutes, that he would never be able to get rid of him and go in search of Old Austinian number three, his bosom friend.

At other intervals, present Austinians of tender years were manoeuvring half-companies of sisters, aunts, and mothers, and trying without much success to pretend that they did not belong to them. A pretence which came down heavily when one of the aunts addressed them as 'Willie' or 'Phil', and wanted to know audibly if 'that boy who had just passed' (*the* one person in the School whom they happened to hate and despise) was their best friend. It was a little trying, too, to have to explain in the middle of a crowd that the reason why you were not running in 'that race' (the 'under thirteen' hundred, by Jove, which ought to have been a gift to you, only, etc.) was because you had been ignominiously knocked out in the trial heats.

In short, the afternoon wore on. Welch won the hundred by two yards and the quarter by twenty, and the other events fell in nearly every case to the favourite. The hurdles created something of a surprise – Jackson, who ought to have won, coming down over the last hurdle but two, thereby enabling Dallas to pull off an unexpected victory by a couple of yards. Vaughan's enthusiastic watch made the time a little under sixteen seconds, but the official timekeeper had other views. There were no instances of the timid new boy, at whom previously the world had scoffed, walking away with the most important race of the day.

And then the spectators were roused from a state of coma by the sound of the bell ringing for the mile. Old Austinian number one gratefully seized the opportunity to escape from Old Austinian number two, and lose himself in the crowd. Young Pounceby-Green with equal gratitude left his father talking to the Head, and shot off without ceremony to get a good place at the ropes. In fact, there was a general stir of anticipation, and all round the ring paterfamilias was asking his son and heir which was Drake and which Thomson, and settling his glasses more firmly on the bridge of his nose.

The staff of *The Glow Worm* conducted Jim to the starting-place, and did their best to relieve his obvious nervousness with light conversation.

'Eh, old chap?' said Jim. He had been saying 'Eh?' to everything throughout the afternoon.

'I said, "Is my hat on straight, and does it suit the colour of my eyes?"' said Charteris.

'Oh, yes. Yes, rather. Ripping,' in a far-off voice.

'And have you a theory of the Universe?'

'Eh, old chap?'

'I said, "Did you want your legs rubbed before you start?" I believe it's an excellent specific for the gout.'

'Gout? What? No, I don't think so, thanks.'

'And you'll write to us sometimes, Jim, and give my love to little Henry, and *always* wear flannel next your skin, my dear boy?' said Charteris.

This seemed to strike even Jim as irrelevant.

'Do shut up for goodness sake, Alderman,' he said irritably. 'Why can't you go and rag somebody else?'

'My place is by your side. Go, my son, or else they'll be starting without you. Give us your blazer. And take my tip, the tip of an old runner, and don't pocket your opponent's ball in your own twenty-five. And come back victorious, or on the shields of your soldiers. All right, sir (to the starter), he's just making his will. Good-bye Jim. Buck up, or I'll lynch you after the race.'

Jim answered by muffling him in his blazer, and walking to the line. There were six competitors in all, each of whom owned a name ranking alphabetically higher than Thomson. Jim, therefore, had the outside berth. Drake had the one next to the inside, which fell to Adamson, the victim of the lost two pounds episode.

Both Drake and Jim got off well at the sound of the pistol, and the pace was warm from the start. Jim evidently had his eye on the inside berth, and, after half a lap had been completed, he got it, Drake falling back. Jim continued to make the running, and led at the end of the first lap by about five yards. Then came Adamson, followed by a batch of three, and finally Drake, taking things exceedingly coolly, a couple of yards behind them. The distance separating him from Jim was little over a dozen yards. A roar of applause greeted the runners as they started on the second lap, and it was significant that while Jim's supporters shouted, 'Well run', those of Drake were fain to substitute advice for approval, and cry 'Go it'. Drake, however, had not the least intention of 'going it' in the generally accepted meaning of the phrase. A yard or two to the rear meant nothing in the first lap, and he was running quite well enough to satisfy himself, with a nice, springy stride, which he hoped would begin to tell soon.

With the end of the second lap the real business of the race began, for the survival of the fittest had resulted in eliminations and changes of order. Jim still led, but now by only eight or nine yards. Drake had come up to second, and Adamson had dropped to a bad third. Two of the runners had given the race up, and retired, and the last man was a long way behind, and, to all practical purposes, out of the running. There were only three laps, and, as the last lap began, the pace quickened, fast as it had been before. Jim was exerting every particle of his strength. He was not a runner who depended overmuch on his final dash. He hoped to gain so much ground before Drake made his sprint as to neutralize it when it came. Adamson he did not fear.

And now they were in the last two hundred yards, Jim by this time some thirty yards ahead, but in great straits. Drake had quickened his pace, and gained slowly on him. As they rounded the corner and came into the straight, the cheers were redoubled. It was a great race. Then, fifty yards from the tape, Drake began his final sprint. If he had saved himself before, he made up for it now. The gap dwindled and dwindled. Neither could improve his pace. It was a question whether there was enough of the race left for Drake to catch his man, or whether he had once more left his sprint till too late. Jim could hear the roars of the spectators, and the frenzied appeals of Merevale's House to him to sprint, but he was already doing his utmost. Everything seemed black to him, a black, surging mist, and in its centre a thin white line, the tape. Could he reach it before Drake? Or would he collapse before he reached it? There were only five more yards to go now, and still he led. Four. Three. Two. Then something white swept past him on the right, the white line quivered, snapped, and vanished, and he pitched blindly forward on to the turf at the track-side. Drake had won by a foot.

12 AN INTERESTING INTERVIEW

For the rest of the afternoon Jim had a wretched time. To be beaten after such a race by a foot, and to be beaten by a foot when victory would have cut the Gordian knot of his difficulties once and for all, was enough to embitter anybody's existence. He found it hard to accept the well-meant condolences of casual acquaintances, and still harder to do the right thing and congratulate Drake on his victory, a refinement of self-torture which is by custom expected of the vanquished in every branch of work or sport. But he managed it somehow, and he also managed to appear reasonably gratified when he went up to take his prize for the half-mile. Tony and the others, who knew what his defeat meant to him, kept out of his way, for which he was grateful. After lock-up, however, it was a different matter, but by that time he was more ready for society. Even now there might be some way out of the difficulty. He asked Tony's advice on the subject. Tony was perplexed. The situation was beyond his grip.

'I don't see what you can do, Jim,' he said, 'unless the Rugby chap'll be satisfied with a pound on account. It's a beastly business. Do you think your pater will give you your money all the same as it was such a close finish?'

Jim thought not. In fact, he was certain that he would not, and Tony relapsed into silence as he tried to bring another idea to the surface. He had not succeeded when Charteris came in.

'Jim,' he said, 'you have my sympathy. It was an awfully near thing. But I've got something more solid than sympathy. I will take a seat.'

'Don't rag, Charteris,' said Tony. 'It's much too serious.'

'Who's ragging, you rotter? I say I have something more solid than sympathy, and instead of giving me an opening, as a decent individual would, by saying, "What?" you accuse me of ragging. James, my son, if you will postpone your suicide for two minutes, I will a tale unfold. I have an idea.'

'Well?'

'That's more like it. Now you *are* talking. We will start at the beginning. First, you want a pound. So do I. Secondly, you want it before next Tuesday. Thirdly, you haven't it on you. How, therefore, are you to get it? As the song hath it, you don't know, they don't know, but – now we come to the point – I *do* know.'

'Yes?' said Jim and Tony together.

'It is a luminous idea. Why shouldn't we publish a special number of *The Glow Worm* before the end of term?'

Jim was silent at the brilliance of the scheme. Then doubts began to harass him.

'Is there time?'

'Time? Yards of it. This is Saturday. We start tonight, and keep at it all night, if necessary. We ought to manage it easily before tomorrow morning. On Sunday we jellygraph it – it'll have to be a jellygraphed number this time. On Monday and Tuesday we sell it, and there you are.'

'How are you going to sell it? In the ordinary way at the shop?'

'Yes, I've arranged all that. All we've got to do is to write the thing. As the penalty for your sins you shall take on most of it.

I'll do the editorial, Welch is pegging away at the Sports account now, and I waylaid Jackson just before lock-up, and induced him by awful threats to knock off some verses. So we're practically published already.'

'It's grand,' said Jim. 'And it's awfully decent of you chaps to fag yourselves like this for me. I'll start on something now.'

'But can you raise a sovereign on one number?' asked Tony.

'Either that, or I've arranged with the shop to give us a quid down, and take all profits on this and the next number. They're as keen as anything on the taking-all-profits idea, but I've kept that back to be used only in case of necessity. But the point is that Jim gets his sovereign in any case. I must be off to my editorial. So long,' and he went.

'Grand man, Charteris,' said Tony, as he leant back in his chair in search of a subject. 'You'd better weigh in with an account of the burglary. It's a pity you can't give the realistic description you gave us. It would sell like anything.'

'Wouldn't do to risk it.'

At that moment the door swung violently open, with Merevale holding on to the handle, and following it in its course. Merevale very rarely knocked at a study door, a peculiarity of his which went far towards shattering the nervous systems of the various inmates, who never knew when it was safe to stop work and read fiction.

'Ah, Thomson,' he said, 'I was looking for you. The Headmaster wants to see you over at his House, if you are feeling well enough after your exertions. *Very* close thing, that mile. I don't know when I have seen a better-run race on the College grounds. I suppose you are feeling pretty tired, eh?'

'I am rather, sir, but I had better see the Head. Will he be in his study, sir?'

'Yes, I think so.'

Jim took his cap and went off, while Merevale settled down to spend the evening in Tony's study, as he often did when the term's work was over, and it was no longer necessary to keep up the pretence of preparation.

Parker, the Head's butler, conducted Jim into the presence.

'Sit down, Thomson,' said the Head.

Jim took a seat, and he had just time to notice that his namesake, Mr Thompson, was also present, and that, in spite of the fact that his tie had crept up to the top of his collar, he was looking quite unnecessarily satisfied with himself, when he became aware that the Head was speaking to him.

'I hope you are not feeling any bad effects from your race, Thomson?'

Jim was half inclined to say that his effects were *nil*, but he felt that the quip was too subtle, and would be lost on his present audience, so he merely said that he was not. There was a rather awkward silence for a minute. Then the Head coughed, and said:

'Thomson.'

'Yes, sir.'

'I think it would be fairest to you to come to the point at once, and to tell you the reason why I wished to see you.'

Jim ran over the sins which shot up in his mind like rockets as he heard these ominous words, and he knew that this must be the matter of the Pavilion. He was, therefore, in a measure prepared for the Head's next words.

'Thomson.'

'Yessir.'

'A very serious charge has been brought against you. You are accused of nothing less than this unfortunate burglary of the prizes for the Sports.'

'Yes, sir. Is my accuser Mr Thompson?'

The Headmaster hesitated for a moment, and Mr Thompson spoke. 'That is so,' he said.

'Yes,' said the Head, 'the accusation is brought by Mr Thompson.'

'Yes, sir,' said Jim again, and this time the observation was intended to convey the meaning, 'My dear, good sir, when you've known him as long as I have, you won't mind what Mr Thompson says or does. It's a kind of way he's got, and if he's not under treatment for it, he ought to be.'

'I should like to hear from your own lips that the charge is groundless.'

'Anything to oblige,' thought Jim. Then aloud, 'Yes, sir.'

'You say it is groundless?' This from Mr Thompson.

'Yes, sir.'

'I must warn you, Thomson, that the evidence against you is very strong indeed,' said the Head. 'Without suggesting that you are guilty of this thing, I think I ought to tell you that if you have any confession to make, it will be greatly, very greatly, to your own advantage to make it at once.'

'And give myself away, free, gratis and for nothing,' thought Jim. 'Not for me, thank you.'

'Might I hear Mr Thompson's evidence, sir?' he asked.

'Certainly, Thomson.' He effected a movement in Mr Thompson's direction, midway between a bow and a nod.

Mr Thompson coughed. Jim coughed, too, in the same key. This put Mr Thompson out, and he had to cough again.

'In the first place,' he began, 'it has been conclusively proved that the burglary was the work of an unskilful hand.'

'That certainly seems to point to me as the author,' said Jim flippantly.

'Silence, Thomson,' said the Head, and counsel for the prosecution resumed.

'In the second place, it has been proved that you were at the time of the burglary in great need of money.'

This woke Jim up. It destroyed that feeling of coolness with which he had started the interview. Awful thoughts flashed across his mind. Had he been seen at the time of his burglarious entry? At any rate, how did Mr Thompson come to know of his pecuniary troubles?

'Did you say it had been proved, sir?'

'Yes.'

'How, sir?'

He felt the question was a mistake as he was uttering it. Your really injured innocent would have called all the elements to witness that he was a millionaire. But it was too late to try that now. And, besides, he really did want to know how Mr Thompson had got to hear of this skeleton in his cupboard.

The Headmaster interrupted hurriedly. 'It is a very unfortunate affair altogether, and this is quite the most unfortunate part. A letter came to the College addressed to J. Thomson, and Mr Thompson opened and read it inadvertently. Quite inadvertently.'

'Yes, sir,' said Jim, in a tone which implied, 'I am no George Washington myself, but when you say he read it inadvertently, well—'

'This letter was signed "Allen"—'

'My brother, sir.'

'Exactly. And it asked for two pounds. Evidently in payment of a debt, and the tone of the letter certainly seemed to show that you were not then in possession of the money.'

'Could I have the letter, sir?' Then with respectful venom to

Mr Thompson: 'If you have finished with it.' The letter was handed over, and pocketed, and Jim braced his moral pecker up for the next round of the contest.

'I take it, then, Thomson,' resumed the Head, 'that you owe your brother this money?'

'Yes, sir.'

'Two pounds is a great deal of money for one boy to lend another.'

'It was not lent, sir. It was a bet.'

'A bet!' in a nasty tone from the Head.

'A bet!' in a sepulchral echo from Mr Thompson.

There was a long pause.

'At any other time,' said the Head, 'I should feel it my duty to take serious notice of this, but beside this other matter with which you are charged, it becomes trivial. I can only repeat that the circumstances are exceedingly suspicious, and I think it would be in your interests to tell us all you know without further delay.'

'You take it for granted I am guilty, sir,' began Jim hotly.

'I say that the circumstances seems to point to it. In the first place, you were in need of money. You admit that?'

'Yes, sir.'

'In the second place,' said the Head slowly, 'in the second place, I am told that you were nowhere to be found in the House at half-past eight on the night of the burglary, when you ought certainly to have been in your study at your work.'

Bombshell number two, and a worse one than the first. For the moment Jim's head swam. If he had been asked just then in so many words where he had been at that time, it is likely that he would have admitted everything. By some miracle the Head did not press his point.

'You may go now, Thomson,' he said. 'I should like to see you after morning school on Monday. Good-night.'

'Good-night, sir,' said Jim, and went without another word. Coming so soon after the exertion and strain of the mile, this shock made him feel sick and dizzy.

When he had gone, the Head turned to Mr Thompson with a worried look on his face. 'I feel as certain as I do of anything,' he said thoughtfully, 'that that boy is telling the truth. If he had been guilty, he would not have behaved like that. I feel sure of it.'

Mr Thompson looked equally thoughtful. 'The circumstances are certainly very suspicious,' he said, echoing the Head's own words. 'I wish I could think he was innocent, but I am bound to say I do not. I regard the evidence as conclusive.'

'Circumstantial evidence is proverbially uncertain, Mr Thompson. That is principally the reason why I was so bent on making him confess if he had anything to confess. I can't expel a boy and ruin his whole career on mere suspicion. The matter must be proved, doubly proved, and even then I should feel uneasy until he owned himself guilty. It is a most unpleasant affair, a terrible affair.'

'Most,' agreed Mr Thompson.

And exactly the same thing was occurring at that moment to Jim, as he sat on his bed in his dormitory, and pondered hopelessly on this new complication that had presented itself so unexpectedly. He was getting very near to the end of his tether, was J. Thomson of Merevale's. It seemed to him, indeed, that he had reached it already. Possibly if he had had a clearer conscience and a larger experience, he might have recognized that the evidence which Mr Thompson had described as conclusive, was in reality not strong enough to hang a cat on. Unfortunately, he did not enjoy those advantages.

13 SIR ALFRED SCORES

Soon after Jim had taken his departure, Mr Thompson, after waiting a few minutes in case the Headmaster had anything more to say, drifted silently out of the room. The Head, like the gentleman in the ballad, continued to wear a worried look. The more he examined the matter, the less did he know what to make of it. He believed, as he had said to Mr Thompson, that Jim was entirely innocent. It was an incredible thing, he thought, that a public school boy, a School-prefect, too, into the bargain, should break out of his House and into a cricket pavilion, however great a crisis his finances might be undergoing. And then to steal two of the prizes for the Sports. Impossible. Against this, however, must be placed the theft of the two pounds. It might occur to a boy, as indeed Mr Thompson had suggested, to steal the cups in order to give the impression that a practised burglar had been at work. There was certainly something to be said in favour of this view. But he would never believe such a thing. He was a good judge of character – a headmaster generally is – and he thought he could tell when a boy was speaking the truth and when he was not.

His reflections were interrupted by a knock at the door. The butler entered with a card on a tray. 'Sir Alfred Venner, M.P., Badgwick Hall', said – almost shouted – the card. He read the words without any apparent pleasure.

'Is Sir Alfred here himself, Parker?' he said.

'He is, sir.'

The Headmaster sighed inaudibly but very wearily. He was feeling worried already, and he knew from experience that a *tête-à-tête* with Sir Alfred Venner, M.P., of Badgwick Hall, would worry him still more.

The Head was a man who tried his very hardest to like each and all of his fellow-creatures, but he felt bound to admit that he liked most people a great, a very great, deal better than he liked the gentleman who had just sent in his card. Sir Alfred's manner always jarred upon him. It was so exactly the antithesis of his own. He was quiet and dignified, and addressed everybody alike, courteously. Sir Alfred was restless and fussy. His manner was always dictatorial and generally rude. When he had risen in the House to make his maiden speech, calling the attention of the Speaker to what he described as 'a thorough draught', he had addressed himself with such severity to that official, that a party of Siamese noblemen, who, though not knowing a word of English, had come to listen to the debate, had gone away with the impression that he was the prime minister. No wonder the Headmaster sighed.

'Show him in, Parker,' said he resignedly.

'Yessir.'

Parker retired, leaving the Head to wonder what his visitor's grievance might be this time. Sir Alfred rarely called without a grievance, generally connected with the trespassing of the School on his land.

'Good-evening, Sir Alfred,' he said, as his visitor whirled into the room.

'O-o-o, this sort of thing won't do, you know, Mr Perceval,' said Sir Alfred fussily, adjusting a pair of gold pince-nez on his nose. The Head's name, which has not before been mentioned, was the Reverend Herbert Perceval, M.A. He had shivered at the sound of the 'O-o-o' which had preceded Sir Alfred's remark. He knew, as did other unfortunate people, that the great man was at his worst when he said 'O-o-o'. In moments of comparative calm he said 'Er'.

'I can't put up with it, you know, Mr Perceval. It's too much. A great deal too much.'

'You refer to—?' suggested the Head, with a patience that did him credit.

'This eternal trespassing and tramping in and out of my grounds all day.'

'You have been misinformed, I fear, Sir Alfred. I have not trespassed in your grounds for – ah – a considerable time.' The Head could not resist this thrust. In his unregenerate 'Varsity days he had been a power at the Union, where many a foeman had exposed himself to a verbal counter from him with disastrous results. Now the fencing must be done with buttons on the foils.

'You – what – I don't follow you, Mr Perceval.'

'I understand you to reproach me for trespassing and – ah – tramping in and out of your grounds all day. Was that not your meaning?'

Sir Alfred almost danced with impatience.

'No, no, no. You misunderstand me. You don't follow my drift.'

'In that case, I beg your pardon. I gathered from the extreme severity of your attitude towards me that I was the person to whom you referred.'

'No, no, no. I've come here to complain of your boys.'

It occurred to the Head to ask if the complaint embraced the entire six hundred of them, or merely referred to one of them. But he reflected that the longer he fenced, the longer his visitor would stay. And he decided, in spite of the illicit pleasure to be derived from the exercise, that it was not worth while.

'Ah,' he said.

'Yes,' continued Sir Alfred, 'my keepers tell me the woods were full of them, sir.'

The Head suggested that possibly the keepers had exaggerated.

'Possibly. Possibly they may have exaggerated. But that is not the point. The nuisance is becoming intolerable, Mr Perceval, perfectly intolerable. It is time to take steps.'

'I have already done all that can be done. I have placed your land out of bounds, considerably out of bounds indeed. And I inflict the severest penalties when a breach of the rule is reported to me.'

'It's not enough. It's not nearly enough.'

'I can scarcely do more, I fear, Sir Alfred. There are more than six hundred boys at St Austin's, and it is not within my power to place them all under my personal supervision.'

Here the Head, who had an eye to the humorous, conjured up a picture of six hundred Austinians going for walks, two and two, the staff posted at intervals down the procession, and himself bringing up the rear. He made a mental mem. to laugh when his visitor had retired.

'H'm,' said the baffled M.P. thoughtfully, adjusting his pince-nez once more. ''M no. No, perhaps not. But' – here he brightened up – 'you can punish them when they do trespass.'

'That is so, Sir Alfred. I can and invariably do.'

'Then punish that what's-his-name, Plinkett, Plunkett – I've got the name down somewhere. Yes, Plunkett. I thought so. Punish Plunkett.'

'Plunkett!' said the Head, taken completely by surprise. He, in common with the rest of the world, had imagined Plunkett to be a perfect pattern of what should be. A headmaster, like other judges of character, has his failures.

'Plunkett. Yes, that is the name. Boy with spectacles. Good gracious, Mr Perceval, don't tell me the boy gave me a false name.'

'No. His name is Plunkett. Am I to understand that he was trespassing on your land? Surely there is some mistake? The boy's a School-prefect.'

Here it suddenly flashed upon his mind that he had used that expression before in the course of the day, on the occasion when Mr Thompson first told him of his suspicions in connection with Jim. 'Why, Mr Thompson, the boy's a School-prefect,' had been his exact words. School-prefects had been in his eyes above suspicion. It is a bad day for a school when they are not so. Had that day arrived for St Austin's? he asked himself.

'He may be a School-prefect, Mr Perceval, but the fact remains that he is a trespasser, and ought from your point of view to be punished for breaking bounds.'

The Head suddenly looked almost cheerful again.

'Of course,' he said, 'of course. I thought that there must be an explanation. The rules respecting bounds, Sir Alfred, do not apply to School-prefects, only to the rest of the School.'

'Indeed?' said Sir Alfred. His tone should have warned the Head that something more was coming, but it did not. He continued.

'Of course it was very wrong of him to trespass on your land, but I have no doubt that he did it quite unintentionally. I will speak to him, and I think I can guarantee that he will not do it again.'

'Oh,' said his visitor. 'That is very gratifying, I am sure. Might

I ask, Mr Perceval, if School-prefects at St Austin's have any other privileges?'

The Head began to look puzzled. There was something in his visitor's manner which suggested unpleasant possibilities.

'A few,' he replied. 'They have a few technical privileges, which it would be a matter of some little time to explain.'

'It must be very pleasant to be a prefect at St Austin's,' said Sir Alfred nastily. 'Very pleasant indeed. Might I ask, Mr Perceval, if the technical privileges to which you refer include – smoking?'

The Head started as if, supposing such a thing possible, someone had pinched him. He did not know what to make of the question. From the expression on his face his visitor did not appear to be perpetrating a joke.

'No,' he said sharply, 'they do not include smoking.'

'I merely asked because this was found by my keeper on the boy when he caught him.'

He produced a small silver match-box. The Head breathed again. The reputation of the School-prefect, though shaky, was still able to come up to the scratch.

'A match-box is scarcely a proof that a boy has been smoking, I think,' said he. 'Many boys carry matches for various purposes, I believe. I myself, though a non-smoker, frequently place a box in my pocket.'

For answer Sir Alfred laid a bloated and exceedingly vulgar-looking plush tobacco-pouch on the table beside the match-box.

'That also,' he observed, 'was found in his pocket by my keeper.'

He dived his hand once more into his coat. 'And also this,' he said.

And, with the air of a card-player who trumps his opponent's ace, he placed on the pouch a pipe. And, to make the matter, if possible, worse, the pipe was not a new pipe. It was caked within and coloured without, a pipe that had seen long service. The only mitigating circumstance that could possibly have been urged in favour of the accused, namely that of 'first offence', had vanished.

'It is pleasant,' said Sir Alfred with laborious sarcasm, 'to find a trespasser doing a thing which has caused the dismissal of several keepers. Smoking in my woods I – will – not – permit. I will not have my property burnt down while I can prevent it. Good-evening, Mr Perceval.' With these words he made a dramatic exit.

For some minutes after he had gone the Head remained where he stood, thinking. Then he went across the room and touched the bell.

'Parker,' he said, when that invaluable officer appeared, 'go across to Mr Ward's House, and tell him I wish to see Plunkett. Say I wish to see him at once.'

'Yessir.'

After ten minutes had elapsed, Plunkett entered the room, looking nervous.

'Sit down, Plunkett.'

Plunkett collapsed into a seat. His eye had caught sight of the smoking apparatus on the table.

The Head paced the room, something after the fashion of the tiger at the Zoo, whose clock strikes lunch.

'Plunkett,' he said, suddenly, 'you are a School-prefect.'

'Yes, sir,' murmured Plunkett. The fact was undeniable.

'You know the duties of a School-prefect?'

'Yes, sir.'

'And yet you deliberately break one of the most important rules of the School. How long have you been in the habit of smoking?'

Plunkett evaded the question.

'My father lets me smoke, sir, when I'm at home.'

(A hasty word in the reader's ear. If ever you are accused

of smoking, please – for my sake, if not for your own – try to refrain from saying that your father lets you do it at home. It is a fatal mistake.)

At this, to employ a metaphor, the champagne of the Head's wrath, which had been fermenting steadily during his late interview, got the better of the cork of self-control, and he exploded. If the Mutual Friend ever has grandchildren he will probably tell them with bated breath the story of how the Head paced the room, and the legend of the things he said. But it will be some time before he will be able to speak about it with any freedom. At last there was a lull in the storm.

'I am not going to expel you, Plunkett. But you cannot come back after the holidays. I will write to your father to withdraw you.' He pointed to the door. Plunkett departed in level time.

'What did the Old 'Un want you for?' asked Dallas, curiously, when he returned to the study.

Plunkett had recovered himself by this time sufficiently to be able to tell a lie.

'He wanted to tell me he'd heard from my father about my leaving.'

'About your leaving!' Dallas tried to keep his voice as free as possible from triumphant ecstasy.

'Are you leaving? When?'

'This term.'

'Oh!' said Dallas. It was an uncomfortable moment. He felt that at least some conventional expression of regret ought to proceed from him.

'Don't trouble to lie about being sorry,' said Plunkett with a sneer.

'Thanks,' said Dallas, gratefully, 'since you mention it, I rather think I won't.'

Vaughan came up soon afterwards, and Dallas told him the great news. They were neither of them naturally vindictive, but the Mutual Friend had been a heavy burden to them during his stay in the House, and they did not attempt to conceal from themselves their unfeigned pleasure at the news of his impending departure.

'I'll never say another word against Mr Plunkett, senior, in my life,' said Vaughan. 'He's a philanthropist. I wonder what the Mutual's going to do? Gentleman of leisure, possibly. Unless he's going to the 'Varsity.'

'Same thing, rather. I don't know a bit what he's going to do, and I can't say I care much. He's going, that's the main point.'

'I say,' said Vaughan. 'I believe the Old Man was holding a sort of reception tonight. I know he had Thomson over to his House. Do you think there's a row on?'

'Oh, I don't know. Probably only wanted to see if he was all right after the mile. By Jove, it was a bit of a race, wasn't it?' And the conversation drifted off into matters athletic.

There were two persons that night who slept badly. Jim lay awake until the College clock had struck three, going over in his mind the various points of his difficulties, on the chance of finding a solution of them. He fell asleep at a quarter past, without having made any progress. The Head, also, passed a bad night.

He was annoyed for many reasons, principally, perhaps, because he had allowed Sir Alfred Venner to score so signal a victory over him. Besides that, he was not easy in his mind about Jim. He could not come to a decision. The evidence was all against him, but evidence is noted for its untrustworthiness. The Head would have preferred to judge the matter from his knowledge of Jim's character. But after the Plunkett episode he mistrusted his powers in that direction. He thought the matter over for a time, and then, finding himself unable to sleep, got up and wrote an article for a leading review on the subject of the Doxology. The article was subsequently rejected – which proves that Providence is not altogether incapable of a kindly action – but it served its purpose by sending its author to sleep.

Barrett, too, though he did not allow it to interfere with his slumbers, was considerably puzzled as to what he ought to do about the cups which he had stumbled upon in the wood. He scarcely felt equal to going to the Dingle again to fetch them, and yet every minute he delayed made the chances of their remaining there more remote. He rather hoped that Reade would think of some way out of it. He had a great respect for Reade's intellect, though he did not always show it.

The next day was the day of the Inter-House cross-country race. It was always fixed for the afternoon after Sports Day, a most inconvenient time for it, as everybody who had exerted or over-exerted himself the afternoon before was unable to do himself justice. Today, contrary to general expectation, both Drake and Thomson had turned out. The knowing ones, however, were prepared to bet anything you liked (except cash), that both would drop out before the first mile was over. Merevale's pinned their hopes on Welch. At that time Welch had not done much long-distance running. He confined himself to the hundred yards and the quarter. But he had it in him to do great things, as he proved in the following year, when he won the half, and would have beaten the great Mitchell-Jones record for the mile, but for an accident, or rather an event, which prevented his running. The tale of which is told elsewhere.

The course for the race was a difficult one. There were hedges and brooks to be negotiated, and, worst of all, ploughed fields. The first ploughed field usually thinned the ranks of the competitors considerably. The distance was about ten miles.

The race started at three o'clock. Jim and Welch, Merevale's first string, set the pace from the beginning, and gradually drew away from the rest. Drake came third, and following him the rest of the Houses in a crowd.

Welch ran easily and springily; Jim with more effort. He felt from the start that he could not last. He resolved to do his best for the honour of the House, but just as the second mile was beginning, the first of the ploughed fields appeared in view, stretching, so it appeared to Jim, right up to the horizon. He groaned.

'Go on, Welch,' he gasped. 'I'm done.'

Welch stopped short in his stride, and eyed him critically.

'Yes,' he said, 'better get back to the House. You overdid it yesterday. Lie down somewhere. G'bye.' And he got into his stride again. Jim watched his figure diminish, until at last it was a shapeless dot of white against the brown surface. Then he lay down on his back and panted.

It was in this attitude that Drake found him. For a moment an almost irresistible wish seized him to act in the same way. There was an unstudied comfort about Jim's pose which appealed to him strongly. His wind still held out, but his legs were beginning to feel as if they did not belong to him at all. He pulled up for an instant.

'Hullo,' he said, 'done up?'

For reply Jim merely grunted.

'Slacker,' said Drake. 'Where's Welch?'

'Miles ahead.'

'Oh Lord!' groaned Drake and, pulling himself together, set out painfully once more across the heavy surface of the field.

Jim lay where he was a little longer. The recollection of the other runners, who might be expected to arrive shortly, stirred him to action. He did not wish to interview everyone on the subject of his dropping out. He struck off at right angles towards the hedge on the left. As he did so, the first of the crowd entered the field. Simpson *major*, wearing the colours of Perkins's House on his manly bosom, was leading. Behind him came a group of four, two School House, Dallas of Ward's, and a representative of Prater's. A minute later they were followed by a larger group, consisting this time of twenty or more runners – all that was left of the fifty who had started. The rest had dropped out at the sight of the ploughed field.

Jim watched the procession vanish over the brow of the hill, and, as it passed out of sight, began to walk slowly back to the School again.

He reached it at last, only to find it almost entirely deserted. In Merevale's House there was nobody. He had hoped that Charteris and Tony might have been somewhere about. When he had changed into his ordinary clothes, he made a tour of the School grounds. The only sign of life, as far as he could see, was Biffen, who was superintending the cutting of the grass on the cricket-field. During the winter Biffen always disappeared, nobody knew where, returning at the beginning of Sports Week to begin preparations for the following cricket season. It had been stated that during the winter he shut himself up and lived on himself after the fashion of a bear. Others believed that he went and worked in some Welsh mine until he was needed again at the School. Biffen himself was not communicative on the subject, a fact which led a third party to put forward the awful theory that he was a professional association player and feared to mention his crime in a school which worshipped Rugby.

'Why, Mr Thomson,' he said, as Jim came up, 'I thought you was running. Whoa!' The last remark was addressed to a bored-looking horse attached to the mowing-machine. From the expression on its face, the animal evidently voted the whole process pure foolishness. He pulled up without hesitation, and Biffen turned to Jim again.

'Surely they ain't come back yet?' he said.

'I have,' said Jim. 'I did myself up rather in the mile yesterday, and couldn't keep up the pace. I dropped out at that awfully long ploughed field by Parker's Spinney.'

Biffen nodded.

'And 'oo was winning, sir?'

'Well, Welch was leading, the last I saw of it. Shouldn't wonder if he won either. He was going all right. I say, the place seems absolutely deserted. Isn't anybody about?'

'Just what Mr MacArthur was saying to me just this minute, sir. 'E went into the Pavilion.'

'Good. I'll go and hunt for him.'

Biffen 'clicked' the *blasé* horse into movement again. Jim went to the Pavilion and met the Babe coming down the steps.

'Hullo, Babe! I was looking for you.'

'Hullo! Why aren't you running?'

'Dropped out. Come and have tea in my study.'

'No, I'll tell you what. You come back with me. I've got rather a decent dog I want to show you. Only got him yesterday.'

Jim revelled in dogs, so he agreed instantly. The Babe lived with his parents in a big house about a mile from the College, and in so doing was the object of much envy amongst those who had to put up with life at the Houses. Jim had been to his home once or twice before, and had always had a very good time indeed there. The two strolled off. In another hour the place began to show signs of life again. The School began to return by ones and twos, most of them taking up a position near the big gates. This was where the race was to finish. There was a straight piece of road about two hundred yards in length before the high road was reached. It was a sight worth seeing when the runners, paced by their respective Houses on each side of the road, swept round the corner, and did their best to sprint with all that was left in them after ten miles of difficult country. Suddenly a distant shouting began to be heard. The leaders had been sighted. The noise increased, growing nearer and nearer, until at last it swelled into a roar, and a black mass of runners turned the corner. In the midst of the black was one white figure – Welch, as calm and unruffled as if he had been returning from a short trot to improve his wind. Merevale's surged round him in a cheering mob. Welch simply disregarded them. He knew where he wished to begin his sprint, and he would begin it at that spot and no other. The spot he had chosen was well within a hundred yards from the gates. When he reached it, he let himself go, and from the uproar, the crowd appeared to be satisfied. A long pause, and still none of the other runners appeared. Five minutes went by before they began to appear. First Jones, of the School House, and Simpson, who raced every yard of the way, and finished in the order named, and then three of Philpott's House in a body. The rest dropped in at intervals for the next quarter of an hour.

The Headmaster always made a point of watching the finish

of the cross-country run. Indeed, he was generally one of the last to leave. With the majority of the spectators it was enough to see the first five safely in.

The last man and lock-up arrived almost simultaneously, and the Head went off to a well-earned dinner.

He had just finished this meal, and was congratulating himself on not being obliged to spend the evening in a series of painful interviews, as had happened the night before, when Parker, the butler, entered the room.

'Well, Parker, what is it?' asked he.

'Mr Roberts, sir, wishes to see you.'

For a moment the Head was at a loss. He could not recall any friend or acquaintance of that name. Then he remembered that Roberts was the name of the detective who had come down from London to look into the matter of the prizes.

'Very well,' he said, resignedly, 'show him into the study.'

Parker bowed, and retired. The Head, after an interval, followed him, and made his way to the study.

15 MR ROBERTS EXPLAINS

Inspector Roberts was standing with his back to the door, examining a photograph of the College, when the Head entered. He spun round briskly. 'Good-evening, Mr Roberts. Pray be seated. You wish to see me?'

The detective took a seat.

'This business of the cups, sir.'

'Ah!' said the Head, 'have you made any progress?'

'Considerable. Yes, very considerable progress. I've found out who stole them.'

'You have?' cried the Head. 'Excellent. I suppose it *was* Thomson, then? I was afraid so.'

'Thomson, sir? That was certainly not the name he gave me. Stokes he called himself.'

'Stokes? Stokes? This is curious. Perhaps if you were to describe his appearance? Was he a tall boy, of a rather slight build—'

The detective interrupted.

'Excuse me, sir, but I rather fancy we have different persons in our mind. Stokes is not a boy. Not at all. Well over thirty. Red moustache. Height, five foot seven, I should say. Not more. Works as a farmhand when required, and does odd jobs at times. That's the man.'

The Head's face expressed relief, as he heard this description. 'Then Thomson did not do it after all,' he said.

'Thomson?' queried Mr Roberts.

'Thomson,' explained the Head, 'is the name of one of the boys at the School. I am sorry to say that I strongly suspected him of this robbery.'

'A boy at the School. Curious. Unusual, I should have thought, for a boy to be mixed up in an affair like this. Though I have known cases.'

'I was very unwilling, I can assure you, to suspect him of such a thing, but really the evidence all seemed to point to it. I am afraid, Mr Roberts, that I have been poaching on your preserves without much success.'

'Curious thing evidence,' murmured Mr Roberts, fixing with his eye a bust of Socrates on the writing-desk, as if he wished it to pay particular attention to his words. 'Very curious. Very seldom able to trust it. Case the other day. Man charged with robbery from the person. *With* violence. They gave the case to me. Worked up beautiful case against the man. Not a hitch anywhere. Whole thing practically proved. Man brings forward *alibi*. Proves it. Turned out that at time of robbery he had been serving seven days without the option for knocking down two porters and a guard on the District Railway. Yet the evidence seemed conclusive. Yes, curious thing evidence.' He nodded solemnly at Socrates, and resumed an interested study of the carpet.

The Head, who had made several spirited attempts at speaking during this recital, at last succeeded in getting in a word.

'You have the cups?'

'No. No, cups still missing. Only flaw in the affair. Perhaps I had better begin from the beginning?'

'Exactly. Pray let me hear the whole story. I am more glad

than I can say that Thomson is innocent. There is no doubt of that, I hope?'

'Not the least, sir. Not the very least. Stokes is the man.'

'I am very glad to hear it.'

The inspector paused for a moment, coughed, and drifted into his narrative.

'. . . Saw at once it was not the work of a practised burglar. First place, how could regular professional know that the cups were in the Pavilion at all? Quite so. Second place, work very clumsily done. No neatness. Not the professional touch at all. Tell it in a minute. No mistaking it. Very good. Must, therefore, have been amateur – this night only – and connected with School. Next question, who? Helped a little there by luck. Capital thing luck, when it's not bad luck. Was passing by the village inn – you know the village inn, I dare say, sir?'

The Head, slightly scandalized, explained that he was seldom in the village. The detective bowed and resumed his tale.

'As I passed the door, I ran into a man coming out. In a very elevated, not to say intoxicated, state. As a matter of fact, barely able to stand. Reeled against wall, and dropped handful of money. I lent helping hand, and picked up his money for him. Not my place to arrest drunken men. Constable's! No constable there, of course. Noticed, as I picked the money up, that there was a good deal of it. For ordinary rustic, a *very* good deal. Sovereign and plenty of silver.' He paused, mused for a while, and went on again.

'Yes. Sovereign, and quite ten shillings' worth of silver. Now the nature of my profession makes me a suspicious man. It struck me as curious, not to say remarkable, that such a man should have thirty shillings or more about him so late in the week. And then there was another thing. I thought I'd seen this particular man somewhere on the School grounds. Couldn't recall his face exactly, but just had a sort of general recollection of having seen him before. I happened to have a camera with me. As a matter of fact I had been taking a few photographs of the place. Pretty place, sir.'

'Very,' agreed the Head.

'You photograph yourself, perhaps?'

'No. I – ah – do not.'

'Ah. Pity. Excellent hobby. However – I took a snap-shot of this man to show to somebody who might know him better than I did. This is the photograph. Drunk as a lord, is he not?'

He exhibited a small piece of paper. The Head examined it gravely, and admitted that the subject of the picture did not appear to be ostentatiously sober. The sunlight beat full on his face, which wore the intensely solemn expression of the man who, knowing his own condition, hopes, by means of exemplary conduct, to conceal it from the world. The Head handed the photograph back without further comment.

'I gave the man back his money,' went on Mr Roberts, 'and saw him safely started again, and then I set to work to shadow him. Not a difficult job. He walked very slowly, and for all he seemed to care, the whole of Scotland Yard might have been shadowing him. Went up the street, and after a time turned in at one of the cottages. I marked the place, and went home to develop the photograph. Took it to show the man who looks after the cricket-field.'

'Biffen?'

'Just so, Biffen. Very intelligent man. Given me a good deal of help in one way and another all along. Well, I showed it to him and he said he thought he knew the face. Was almost certain it was one of the men at work on the grounds at the time of the robbery. Showed it to friend of his, the other ground-man. He thought same. That made it as certain as I had any need for. Went off at once to the man's cottage, found him sober, and got the whole thing out of him. But not the cups. He had been meaning to sell them, but had not known where to go. Wanted combination of good price and complete safety. Very hard to find, so had kept cups hidden till further notice.'

Here the Head interrupted.

'And the cups? Where are they?'

'We-e-ll,' said the detective, slowly. 'It is this way. We have only got his word to go on as regards the cups. This man, Stokes, it seems is a notorious poacher. The night after the robbery he took the cups out with him on an expedition in some woods that lie in the direction of Badgwick. I think Badgwick is the name.'

'Badgwick! Not Sir Alfred Venner's woods?'

'Sir Alfred Venner it was, sir. That was the name he mentioned. Stokes appears to have been in the habit of visiting that gentleman's property pretty frequently. He had a regular hiding-place, a sort of store where he used to keep all the game he killed. He described the place to me. It is a big tree on the bank of the stream nearest the high road. The tree is hollow. One has to climb to find the opening to it. Inside are the cups, and, I should say, a good deal of mixed poultry. That is what he told me, sir. I should advise you, if I may say so, to write a note to Sir Alfred Venner, explaining the case, and ask him to search the tree, and send the cups on here.'

This idea did not appeal to the Head at all. Why, he thought bitterly, was this wretched M.P. always mixed up with his affairs? Left to himself, he could have existed in perfect comfort without either seeing, writing to, or hearing from the great man again for the rest of his life. 'I will think it over,' he said, 'though it seems the only thing to be done. As for Stokes, I suppose I must prosecute—'

The detective raised a hand in protest.

'Pardon my interruption, sir, but I really should advise you not to prosecute.'

'Indeed! Why?'

'It is this way. If you prosecute, you get the man his term of imprisonment. A year, probably. Well and good. But then what happens? After his sentence has run out, he comes out of prison an ex-convict. Tries to get work. No good. Nobody will look at him. Asks for a job. People lock up their spoons and shout for the police. What happens then? Not being able to get work, tries another burglary. Being a clumsy hand at the game, gets caught again and sent back to prison, and so is ruined and becomes a danger to society. Now, if he is let off this time, he will go straight for the rest of his life. Run a mile to avoid a silver cup. He's badly scared, and I took the opportunity of scaring him more. Told him nothing would happen this time, if the cups came back safely, but that he'd be watched ever afterwards to see he did not get into mischief. Of course he won't really be watched, you understand, but he thinks he will. Which is better, for it saves trouble. Besides, we know where the cups are – I feel sure he was speaking the truth about them, he was too frightened to invent a story – and here is most of the money. So it all ends well, if I may put it so. My advice, sir, and I think you will find it good advice – is not to prosecute.'

'Very well,' said the Head, 'I will not.'

'Very good, sir. Good-morning, sir.' And he left the room.

The Head rang the bell.

'Parker,' said he, 'go across to Mr Merevale's, and ask him to send Thomson to me.'

It was with mixed feelings that he awaited Jim's arrival. The detective's story had shown how unjust had been his former suspicions, and he felt distinctly uncomfortable at the prospect of the apology which he felt bound to make to him. On the other hand, this feeling was more than equalled by his relief at finding that his faith in the virtue of the *genus* School-prefect, though at fault in the matter of Plunkett, was not altogether misplaced. It made up for a good deal. Then his thoughts drifted to Sir Alfred Venner. Struggle with his feelings as he might, the Head could *not* endure that local potentate. The recent interview between them had had no parallel in their previous acquaintance, but the Head had always felt vaguely irritated by his manner and speech, and he had always feared that matters would come to a head sooner or later. The prospect of opening communication with him once more was not alluring. In the meantime there was his more immediate duty to be performed, the apology to Thomson. But that reminded him. The apology must only be of a certain kind. It must not be grovelling. And this for a very excellent reason. After the apology must come an official lecture on the subject of betting. He had rather lost sight of that offence in the excitement of the greater crime of which Thomson had been accused, and very nearly convicted. Now the full heinousness of it came back to him. Betting! Scandalous!

'Come in,' he cried, as a knock at the door roused him from his thoughts. He turned. But instead of Thomson, there appeared Parker. Parker carried a note. It was from Mr Merevale.

The Head opened it.

'What!' he cried, as he read it. 'Impossible.' Parker made no comment. He stood in the doorway, trying to look as like a piece of furniture as possible – which is the duty of a good butler.

'Impossible!' said the Head again.

What Mr Merevale had said in his note was this, that Thomson was not in the House, and had not been in the House since lunch-time. He ought to have returned at six o'clock. It was now half-past eight, and still there were no signs of him. Mr Merevale expressed a written opinion that this was a remarkable thing, and the Head agreed with him unreservedly.

16 THE DISAPPEARANCE OF J. THOMSON

Certainly the Head was surprised.

He read the note again. No. There was no mistake. 'Thomson is not in the House.' There could be no two meanings about that.

'Go across to Mr Merevale's,' he said at last, 'and ask him if he would mind seeing me here for a moment.'

The butler bowed his head gently, but with more than a touch of pained astonishment. He thought the Headmaster might show more respect for persons. A butler is not an errand-boy.

'Sir?' he said, giving the Head a last chance, as it were, of realizing the situation.

'Ask Mr Merevale to step over here for a moment.'

The poor man bowed once more. The phantom of a half-smoked cigar floated reproachfully before his eyes. He had lit it a quarter of an hour ago in fond anticipation of a quiet evening. Unless a miracle had occurred, it must be out by this time. And he knew as well as anybody else that a relighted cigar is never at its best. But he went, and in a few minutes Mr Merevale entered the room.

'Sit down, Mr Merevale,' said the Head. 'Am I to understand from your note that Thomson is actually not in the House?'

Mr Merevale thought that if he had managed to understand anything else from the note he must possess a mind of no common order, but he did not say so.

'No,' he said. 'Thomson has not been in the House since lunch-time, as far as I know. It is a curious thing.'

'It is exceedingly serious. Exceedingly so. For many reasons. Have you any idea where he was seen last?'

'Harrison in my House says he saw him at about three o'clock.'

'Ah!'

'According to Harrison, he was walking in the direction of Stapleton.'

'Ah. Well, it is satisfactory to know even as little as that.'

'Just so. But Mace – he is in my House, too – declares that he saw Thomson at about the same time cycling in the direction of Badgwick. Both accounts can scarcely be correct.'

'But – dear me, are you certain, Mr Merevale?'

Merevale nodded to imply that he was. The Head drummed irritably with his fingers on the arm of his chair. This mystery, coming as it did after the series of worries through which he had been passing for the last few days, annoyed him as much as it is to be supposed the last straw annoyed the proverbial camel.

'As a matter of fact,' said Merevale, 'I know that Thomson started to run in the long race this afternoon. I met him going to the starting-place, and advised him to go and change again. He was not looking at all fit for such a long run. It seems to me that Welch might know where he is. Thomson and he got well ahead of the others after the start, so that if, as I expect, Thomson dropped out early in the race, Welch could probably tell us where it happened. That would give us some clue to his whereabouts, at any rate.'

'Have you questioned Welch?'

'Not yet. Welch came back very tired, quite tired out, in fact and went straight to bed. I hardly liked to wake him except as a last resource. Perhaps I had better do so now?'

'I think you should most certainly. Something serious must have happened to Thomson to keep him out of his House as late as this. Unless—'

He stopped. Merevale looked up enquiringly. The Head, after a moment's deliberation, proceeded to explain.

'I have made a very unfortunate mistake with regard to Thomson, Mr Merevale. A variety of reasons led me to think that he had had something to do with this theft of the Sports prizes.'

'Thomson!' broke in Merevale incredulously.

'There was a considerable weight of evidence against him, which I have since found to be perfectly untrustworthy, but which at the time seemed to me almost conclusive.'

'But surely,' put in Merevale again, 'surely Thomson would be the last boy to do such a thing. Why should he? What would he gain by it?'

'Precisely. I can understand that perfectly in the light of certain information which I have just received from the inspector. But at the time, as I say, I believed him guilty. I even went so far as to send for him and question him upon the subject. Now it has occurred to me, Mr Merevale – you understand that I put it forward merely as a conjecture – it occurs to me—'

'That Thomson has run away,' said Merevale bluntly.

The Head, slightly discomposed by this Sherlock-Holmes-like reading of his thoughts, pulled himself together, and said, 'Ah – just so. I think it very possible.'

'I do not agree with you,' said Merevale. 'I know Thomson well, and I think he is the last boy to do such a thing. He is neither a fool nor a coward, to put it shortly, and he would need to have a great deal of both in him to run away.'

The Head looked slightly relieved at this.

'You – ah – think so?' he said.

'I certainly do. In the first place, where, unless he went home, would he run to? And as he would be going home in a couple of days in the ordinary course of things, he would hardly be foolish enough to risk expulsion in such a way.'

Mr Merevale always rather enjoyed his straight talks with the Headmaster. Unlike most of his colleagues he stood in no awe of him whatever. He always found him ready to listen to sound argument, and, what was better, willing to be convinced. It was so in this case.

'Then I think we may dismiss that idea,' said the Head with visible relief. The idea of such a scandal occurring at St Austin's had filled him with unfeigned horror. 'And now I think it would be as well to go across to your House and hear what Welch has to say about the matter. Unless Thomson returns soon – and it is already past nine o'clock – we shall have to send out search-parties.'

Five minutes later Welch, enjoying a sound beauty-sleep, began to be possessed of a vague idea that somebody was trying to murder him. His subsequent struggles for life partially woke him, and enabled him to see dimly that two figures were standing by his bed.

'Yes?' he murmured sleepily, turning over on to his side again, and preparing to doze off. The shaking continued. This was too much. 'Look here,' said he fiercely, sitting up. Then he recognized his visitors. As his eye fell on Merevale, he wondered whether anything had occurred to bring down his wrath upon him. Perhaps he had gone to bed without leave, and was being routed out to read at prayers or do some work? No, he remembered distinctly getting permission to turn in. What then could be the matter?

At this point he recognized the Headmaster, and the last mists of sleep left him.

'Yes, sir?' he said, wide-awake now.

Merevale put the case briefly and clearly to him. 'Sorry to disturb you, Welch. I know you are tired.'

'Not at all, sir,' said Welch, politely.

'But there is something we must ask you. You probably do not know that Thomson has not returned?'

'Not returned!'

'No. Nobody knows where he is. You were probably the last to see him. What happened when you and he started for the long run this afternoon? You lost sight of the rest, did you not?'

'Yes, sir.'

'Well?'

'And Thomson dropped out.'

'Ah.' This from the Headmaster.

'Yes, sir. He said he couldn't go any farther. He told me to go on. And, of course, I did, as it was a race. I advised him to go back to the House and change. He looked regularly done up. I think he ran too hard in the mile yesterday.'

The Head spoke.

'I thought that some such thing must have happened. Where was it that he dropped out, Welch?'

'It was just as we came to a long ploughed field, sir, by the side of a big wood.'

'Parker's Spinney, I expect,' put in Merevale.

'Yes, sir. About a mile from the College.'

'And you saw nothing more of him after that?' enquired the Headmaster.

'No, sir. He was lying on his back when I left him. I should think some of the others must have seen him after I did. He didn't look as if he was likely to get up for some time.'

'Well,' said the Head, as he and Merevale went out of the

room, leaving Welch to his slumbers, 'we have gained little by seeing Welch. I had hoped for something more. I must send the prefects out to look for Thomson at once.'

'It will be a difficult business,' said Merevale, refraining – to his credit be it said – from a mention of needles and haystacks. 'We have nothing to go upon. He may be anywhere for all we know. I suppose it is hardly likely that he is still where Welch left him?'

The Head seemed to think this improbable. 'That would scarcely be the case unless he were very much exhausted. It is more than five hours since Welch saw him. I can hardly believe that the worst exhaustion would last so long. However, if you would kindly tell your House-prefects of this—'

'And send them out to search?'

'Yes. We must do all we can. Tell them to begin searching where Thomson was last seen. I will go round to the other Houses. Dear me, this is exceedingly annoying. Exceedingly so.'

Merevale admitted that it was, and, having seen his visitor out of the House, went to the studies to speak to his prefects. He found Charteris and Tony together in the former's sanctum.

'Has anything been heard about Thomson, sir?' said Tony, as he entered.

'That is just what I want to see you about. Graham, will you go and bring the rest of the prefects here?'

'Now,' he said, as Tony returned with Swift and Daintree, the two remaining House-prefects, 'you all know, of course, that Thomson is not in the House. The Headmaster wants you to go and look for him. Welch seems to have been the last to see him, and he left him lying in a ploughed field near Parker's Spinney. You all know Parker's Spinney, I suppose?'

'Yes, sir.'

'Then you had better begin searching from there. Go in twos if you like, or singly. Don't all go together. I want you all to be back by eleven. All got watches?'

'Yes, sir.'

'Good. You'd better take lanterns of some sort. I think I can raise a bicycle lamp each, and there is a good moon. Look everywhere, and shout as much as you like. I think he must have sprained an ankle or something. He is probably lying somewhere unable to move, and too far away from the road to make his voice heard to anyone. If you start now, you will have just an hour and a half. You should have found him by then. The prefects from the other Houses will help you.'

Daintree put in a pertinent question.

'How about trespassing, sir?'

'Oh, go where you like. In reason, you know. Don't go getting the School mixed up in any unpleasantness, of course, but remember that your main object is to find Thomson. You all understand?'

'Yes, sir.'

'Very good. Then start at once.'

'By Jove,' said Swift, when he had gone, 'what an unholy rag! This suits yours truly. Poor old Jim, though. I wonder what the deuce has happened to him?'

At that very moment the Headmaster, leaving Philpott's House to go to Prater's, was wondering the same thing. In spite of Mr Merevale's argument, he found himself drifting back to his former belief that Jim had run away. What else could keep him out of his House more than three hours after lock-up? And he had had some reason for running away, for the *conscia mens recti*, though an excellent institution in theory, is not nearly so useful an ally as it should be in practice. The Head knocked at Prater's door, pondering darkly within himself.

17 ‘WE’LL PROCEED TO SEARCH FOR THOMSON IF HE BE ABOVE THE GROUND’

‘How sweet the moonlight sleeps on yonder haystack,’ observed Charteris poetically, as he and Tony, accompanied by Swift and Daintree, made their way across the fields to Parker’s Spinney. Each carried a bicycle lamp, and at irregular intervals each broke into piercing yells, to the marked discomfort of certain birds roosting in the neighbourhood, who burst noisily from the trees, and made their way with visible disgust to quieter spots.

‘There’s one thing,’ said Swift, ‘we ought to hear him if he yells on a night like this. A yell ought to travel about a mile.’

‘Suppose we try one now,’ said Charteris. ‘Now. A concerted piece, *andante* in six-eight time. Ready?’

The next moment the stillness of the lovely spring night was shattered by a hideous uproar.

‘R.S.V.P.,’ said Charteris to space in general, as the echoes died away. But there was no answer, though they waited several minutes on the chance of hearing some sound that would indicate Jim’s whereabouts.

‘If he didn’t hear that,’ observed Tony, ‘he can’t be within three miles, that’s a cert. We’d better separate, I think.’

They were at the ploughed field by Parker’s Spinney now.

‘Anybody got a coin?’ asked Daintree. ‘Let’s toss for directions.’

Charteris produced a shilling.

'My ewe lamb,' he said. 'Tails.'

Tails it was. Charteris expressed his intention of striking westward and drawing the Spinney. He and Tony made their way thither, Swift and Daintree moving off together in the opposite direction.

'This is jolly rum,' said Tony, as they entered the Spinney. 'I wonder where the deuce the man has got to?'

'Yes. It's beastly serious, really, but I'm hanged if I can help feeling as if I were out on a picnic. I suppose it's the night air.'

'I wonder if we shall find him?'

'Not the slightest chance in my opinion. There's not the least good in looking through this forsaken Spinney. Still, we'd better do it.'

'Yes. Don't make a row. We're trespassing.'

They moved on in silence. Half way through the wood Charteris caught his foot in a hole and fell.

'Hurt?' said Tony.

'Only in spirit, thanks. The absolute dashed foolishness of this is being rapidly borne in upon me, Tony. What *is* the good of it? We shan't find him here.'

Tony put his foot down upon these opinions with exemplary promptitude.

'We must go on trying. Hang it all, if it comes to the worst, it's better than frousting indoors.'

'Tony, you're a philosopher. Lead on, Macduff.'

Tony was about to do so, when a form appeared in front of him, blocking the way. He flashed his lamp at the form, and the form, prefacing its remarks with a good, honest swearword – of a variety peculiar to that part of the country – requested him, without any affectation of ceremonious courtesy, to take his something-or-other lamp out of his (the form's) what's-its-named face, and state his business briefly.

'Surely I know that voice,' said Charteris. 'Archibald, my long-lost brother.'

The keeper failed to understand him, and said so tersely.

'Can you tell *me*,' went on Charteris, 'if you have seen such a thing as a boy in this Spinney lately? We happen to have lost one. An ordinary boy. No special markings. His name is Thomson, on the Grampian Hills—'

At this point the keeper felt that he had had enough. He made a dive for the speaker.

Charteris dodged behind Tony, and his assailant, not observing this, proceeded to lay violent hands upon the latter, who had been standing waiting during the conversation.

'Let go, you fool,' cried he. The keeper's hand had come smartly into contact with his left eye, and from there had taken up a position on his shoulder. In reply the keeper merely tightened his grip.

'I'll count three,' said Tony, 'and—'

The keeper's hand shifted to his collar.

'All right, then,' said Tony between his teeth. He hit up with his left at the keeper's wrist. The hand on his collar loosed its grip. Its owner rushed, and as he came, Tony hit him in the parts about the third waistcoat-button with his right. He staggered and fell. Tony hit very hard when the spirit moved him.

'Come on, man,' said Charteris quickly, 'before he gets his wind again. We mustn't be booked trespassing.'

Tony recognized the soundness of the advice. They were out of the Spinney in two minutes.

'Now,' said Charteris, 'let's do a steady double to the road. This is no place for us. Come on, you man of blood.'

When they reached the road they slowed down to a walk again. Charteris laughed.

'I feel just as if we'd done a murder, somehow. What an ass that fellow was to employ violence. He went down all right, didn't he?'

'Think there'll be a row?'

'No. Should think not. He didn't see us properly. Anyhow, he was interfering with an officer in the performance of his duty. So were we, I suppose. Well, let's hope for the best. Hullo!'

'What's up?'

'All right. It's only somebody coming down the road. Thought it might be the keeper at first. Why, it's Biffen.'

It was Biffen. He looked at them casually as he came up, but stopped short in surprise when he saw who they were.

'Mr Charteris!'

'The same,' said Charteris. 'Enjoying a moonlight stroll, Biffen?'

'But what are you doing out of the 'ouse at this time of night, Mr Charteris?'

'It's this way,' said Tony, 'all the House-prefects have been sent out to look for Thomson. He's not come back.'

'Not come back, sir!'

'No. Bit queer, isn't it? The last anybody saw of him was when he dropped out of the long race near Parker's Spinney.'

'I seen him later than that, Mr Graham. He come on to the grounds while I was mowing the cricket field.'

'Not really? When was that?'

'Four. 'Alf past four, nearly.'

'What became of him?'

''E went off with Mr MacArthur. Mr MacArthur took 'im off 'ome with 'im, I think, sir.'

'By Jove,' said Charteris with enthusiasm. 'Now we are on the track. Thanks awfully, Biffen, I'll remember you in my will. Come on, Tony.'

'Where are you going now?'

'Babe's place, of course. The Babe holds the clue to this business. We must get it out of him. 'Night, Biffen.'

'Good-night, sir.'

Arrived at the Babe's residence, they rang the bell, and, in the interval of waiting for the door to be opened, listened with envy to certain sounds of revelry which filtered through the windows of a room to the right of the porch.

'The Babe seems to be making a night of it,' said Charteris. 'Oh' – as the servant opened the door – 'can we see Mr MacArthur, please?'

The servant looked doubtful on the point.

'There's company tonight, sir.'

'I knew he was making a night of it,' said Charteris to Tony. 'It's not Mr MacArthur we want to see. It's – dash it, what's the Babe's name?'

'Robert, I believe. Wouldn't swear to it.'

'Mr Robert. Is he in?' It seemed to Charteris that the form of this question smacked of Ollendorf. He half expected the servant to say 'No, but he has the mackintosh of his brother's cousin'. It produced the desired effect, however, for after inviting them to step in, the servant disappeared, and the Babe came on the scene, wearing a singularly prosperous expression, as if he had dined well.

'Hullo, you chaps,' he said.

'Sir to you,' said Charteris. 'Look here, Babe, we want to know what you have done with Jim. He was seen by competent witnesses to go off with you, and he's not come back. If you've murdered him, you might let us have the body.'

'Not come back! Rot. Are you certain?'

'My dear chap, every House-prefect on the list has been sent out to look for him. When did he leave here?'

The Babe reflected.

'Six, I should think. Little after, perhaps. Why – oh Lord!'

He broke off suddenly.

'What's up?' asked Tony.

'Why I sent him by a short cut through some woods close by here, and I've only just remembered there's a sort of quarry in the middle of them. I'll bet he's in there.'

'Great Scott, man, what sort of a quarry? I like the calm way the Babe talks of sending unsuspecting friends into quarries. Deep?'

'Not very, thank goodness. Still, if he fell down he might not be able to get up again, especially if he'd hurt himself at all. Half a second. Let me get on some boots, and I'll come out and look. Shan't be long.'

When he came back, the three of them set out for the quarry.

'There you are,' cried the Babe, with an entirely improper pride in his voice, considering the circumstances. 'What did I tell you?' Out of the darkness in front of them came a shout. They recognized the voice at once as Jim's.

Tony uttered a yell of encouragement, and was darting forward to the spot from which the cry had come, when the Babe stopped him. 'Don't do that, man,' he said. 'You'll be over yourself, if you don't look out. It's quite close here.'

He flashed one of the lamps in front of him. The light fell on a black opening in the ground, and Jim's voice sounded once more from the bowels of the earth, this time quite close to where they stood.

'Jim,' shouted Charteris, 'where are you?'

'Hullo,' said the voice, 'who's that? You might lug me out of here.'

'Are you hurt?'

'Twisted my ankle.'

'How far down are you?'

'Not far. Ten feet, about. Can't you get me out?'

'Half a second,' said the Babe, 'I'll go and get help. You chaps had better stay here and talk to him.' He ran off.

'How many of you are there up there?' asked Jim.

'Only Tony and myself,' said Charteris.

'Thought I heard somebody else.'

'Oh, that was the Babe. He's gone off to get help.'

'Oh. When he comes back, wring his neck, and heave him down here,' said Jim. 'I want a word with him on the subject of short cuts. I say, is there much excitement about this?'

'Rather. All the House-prefects are out after you. We've been looking in Parker's Spinney, and Tony was reluctantly compelled to knock out a keeper who tried to stop us. You should have been there. It was a rag.'

'Wish I had been. Hullo, is that the Babe come back?'

It was. The Babe, with his father and a party of friends arrayed in evening dress. They carried a ladder amongst them.

The pungent remarks Jim had intended to address to the Babe had no opportunity of active service. It was not the Babe who carried him up the ladder, but two of the dinner-party. Nor did the Babe have a hand in the carrying of the stretcher. That was done by as many of the evening-dress brigade as could get near enough. They seemed to enjoy it. One of them remarked that it reminded him of South Africa. To which another replied that it was far more like a party of policemen gathering in an 'early drunk' in the Marylebone Road. The procession moved on its stately way to the Babe's father's house, and the last Tony and Charteris saw of Jim, he was the centre of attraction, and appeared to be enjoying himself very much.

Charteris envied him, and did not mind saying so.

'Why can't *I* smash my ankle?' he demanded indignantly of Tony.

He was nearing section five, sub-section three, of his discourse, when they reached Merevale's gates. It was after eleven, but they felt that the news they were bringing entitled them to be a little late. Charteris brought his arguments to a premature end, and Tony rang the bell. Merevale himself opened the door to them.

18 IN WHICH THE AFFAIRS OF VARIOUS PERSONS ARE WOUND UP

'Well,' he said, 'you're rather late. Any luck?'

'We've found him, sir,' said Tony.

'Really? That's a good thing. Where was he?'

'He'd fallen down a sort of quarry place near where MacArthur lives. MacArthur took him home with him to tea, and sent him back by a short cut, forgetting all about the quarry, and Thomson fell in and couldn't get out again.'

'Is he hurt?'

'Only twisted his ankle, sir.'

'Then where is he now?'

'They carried him back to the house.'

'MacArthur's house?'

'Yes, sir.'

'Oh, well, I suppose he will be all right then. Graham, just go across and report to the Headmaster, will you? You'll find him in his study.'

The Head was immensely relieved to hear Tony's narrative. After much internal debate he had at last come to the conclusion that Jim must have run away, and he had been wondering how he should inform his father of the fact.

'You are certain that he is not badly hurt, Graham?' he said, when Tony had finished his story.

'Yes, sir. It's only his ankle.'

'Very good. Good-night, Graham.'

The Head retired to bed that night filled with a virtuous resolve to seek Jim out on the following day, and speak a word in season to him on the subject of crime in general and betting in particular. This plan he proceeded to carry out as soon as afternoon school was over. When, however, he had arrived at the Babe's house, he found that there was one small thing which he had left out of his calculations. He had counted on seeing the invalid alone. On entering the sick-room he found there Mrs MacArthur, looking as if she intended to remain where she sat for several hours – which, indeed, actually was her intention – and Miss MacArthur, whose face and attitude expressed the same, only, if anything, more so. The fact was that the Babe, a very monument of resource on occasions, had, as he told Jim, 'given them the tip not to let the Old Man get at him, unless he absolutely chucked them out, you know'. When he had seen the Headmaster approaching, he had gone hurriedly to Jim's room to mention the fact, with excellent results.

The Head took a seat by the bed, and asked, with a touch of nervousness, after the injured ankle. This induced Mrs MacArthur to embark on a disquisition concerning the ease with which ankles are twisted, from which she drifted easily into a discussion of Rugby football, its merits and demerits. The Head, after several vain attempts to jerk the conversation into other grooves, gave it up, and listened for some ten minutes to a series of anecdotes about various friends and acquaintances of Mrs MacArthur's who had either twisted their own ankles or known people who had twisted theirs. The Head began to forget what exactly he had come to say that afternoon. Jim lay and grinned covertly through it all. When the Head did speak, his first words roused him effectually.

'I suppose, Mrs MacArthur, your son has told you that we have had a burglary at the School?'

'Hang it,' thought Jim, 'this isn't playing the game at all. Why talk shop, especially that particular brand of shop, here?' He wondered if the Head intended to describe the burglary, and then spring to his feet with a dramatic wave of the hand towards him, and say, 'There, Mrs MacArthur, is the criminal! There lies the viper on whom you have lavished your hospitality, the snaky and systematic serpent you have been induced by underhand means to pity. Look upon him, and loathe him. *He* stole the cups!'

'Yes, indeed,' replied Mrs MacArthur, 'I have heard a great deal about it. I suppose you have never found out who it was that did it?'

Jim lay back resignedly. After all, he had not done it, and if the Head liked to say he had, well, let him. *He* didn't care.

'Yes, Mrs MacArthur, we have managed to discover him.'

'And who was it?' asked Mrs MacArthur, much interested.

'Now for it,' said Jim to himself.

'We found that it was a man living in the village, who had been doing some work on the School grounds. He had evidently noticed the value of the cups, and determined to try his hand at appropriating them. He is well known as a poacher in the village, it seems. I think that for the future he will confine himself to that – ah – industry, for he is hardly likely ever to – ah – shine as a professional house-breaker. No.'

'Oh, well, that must be a relief to you, I am sure, Mr Perceval. These poachers are a terrible nuisance. They do frighten the birds so.'

She spoke as if it were an unamiable eccentricity on the part of the poachers, which they might be argued out of, if the matter were put before them in a reasonable manner. The Head agreed with her and rose to go. Jim watched him out of the room and then breathed a deep, satisfying breath of relief. His troubles were at an end.

In the meantime Barrett, who, having no inkling as to the rate at which affairs had been progressing since his visit to the Dingle, still imagined that the secret of the hollow tree belonged exclusively to Reade, himself, and one other, was much exercised in his mind about it. Reade candidly confessed himself baffled by the problem. Give him something moderately straightforward, and he was all right. This secret society and dark lantern style of affair was, he acknowledged, beyond him. And so it came about that Barrett resolved to do the only thing he could think of, and go to the Head about it. But before he had come to this decision, the Head had received another visit from Mr Roberts, as a result of which the table where Sir Alfred Venner had placed Plunkett's pipe and other accessories so dramatically during a previous interview, now bore another burden – the missing cups.

Mr Roberts had gone to the Dingle in person, and, by adroit use of the divinity which hedges a detective, had persuaded a keeper to lead him to the tree where, as Mr Stokes had said, the cups had been deposited.

The Head's first act, on getting the cups, was to send for Welch, to whom by right of conquest they belonged. Welch arrived shortly before Barrett. The Head was just handing him his prizes when the latter came into the room. It speaks well for Barrett's presence of mind that he had grasped the situation and decided on his line of action before Welch went, and the Head turned his attention to him.

'Well, Barrett?' said the Head.

'If you please, sir,' said Barrett, blandly, 'may I have leave to go to Stapleton?'

'Certainly, Barrett. Why do you wish to go?'

This was something of a poser, but Barrett's brain worked quickly.

'I wanted to send a telegram, sir.'

'Very well. But' – with suspicion – 'why did you not ask Mr Philpott? Your House-master can give you leave to go to Stapleton.'

'I couldn't find him, sir.' This was true, for he had not looked.

'Ah. Very well.'

'Thank you, sir.'

And Barrett went off to tell Reade that in some mysterious manner the cups had come back on their own account.

When Jim had congratulated himself that everything had ended happily, at any rate as far as he himself was concerned, he had forgotten for the moment that at present he had only one pound to his credit instead of the two which he needed. Charteris, however, had not. The special number of *The Glow Worm* was due on the following day, and Jim's accident left a considerable amount of 'copy' to be accounted for. He questioned Tony on the subject.

'Look here, Tony, have you time to do any more stuff for *The Glow Worm*?'

'My dear chap,' said Tony, 'I've not half done my own bits. Ask Welch.'

'I asked him just now. He can't. Besides, he only writes at about the rate of one word a minute, and we must get it all in by tonight at bed-time. I'm going to sit up as it is to jellygraph it. What's up?'

Tony's face had assumed an expression of dismay.

'Why,' he said, 'Great Scott, I never thought of it before. If we jellygraph it, our handwriting'll be recognized, and that will give the whole show away.'

Charteris took a seat, and faced this difficulty in all its aspects. The idea had never occurred to him before. And yet it should have been obvious.

'I'll have to copy the whole thing out in copper-plate,' he said desperately at last. 'My aunt, what a job.'

'I'll help,' said Tony. 'Welch will, too, I should think, if you ask him. How many jelly machine things can you raise?'

'I've got three. One for each of us. Wait a bit, I'll go and ask Welch.'

Welch, having first ascertained that the matter really was a pressing one, agreed without hesitation. He had objections to spoiling his sleep without reason, but in moments of emergency he put comfort behind him.

'Good,' said Charteris, when this had been settled, 'be here as soon as you can after eleven. I tell you what, we'll do the thing in style, and brew. It oughtn't to take more than an hour or so. It'll be rather a rag than otherwise.'

'And how about Jim's stuff?' asked Welch.

'I shall have to do that, as you can't. I've done my own bits. I think I'd better start now.' He did, and with success. When he went to bed at half-past ten, *The Glow Worm* was ready in manuscript. Only the copying and printing remained to be done.

Charteris was out of bed and in the study just as eleven struck. Tony and Welch, arriving half-an-hour later, found him hard at work copying out an article of topical interest in a fair, round hand, quite unrecognizable as his own.

It was an impressive scene. The gas had been cut off, as it always was when the House went to bed, and they worked by the light of candles. Occasionally Welch, breathing heavily in his efforts to make his handwriting look like that of a member of a board-school (second standard), blew one or more of the candles out, and the others grunted fiercely. That was all they could do, for, for evident reasons, a vow of silence had been imposed. Charteris was the first to finish. He leant back in his chair, and the chair, which at a reasonable hour of the day would have endured any treatment, collapsed now with a noise like a pistol-shot.

'Now you've done it,' said Tony, breaking all rules by speaking considerably above a whisper.

Welch went to the door, and listened. The House was still. They settled down once more to work. Charteris lit the spirit-lamp, and began to prepare the meal. The others toiled painfully on at their round-hand. They finished almost simultaneously.

'Not another stroke do I do,' said Tony, 'till I've had something to drink. Is that water boiling yet?'

It was at exactly a quarter past two that the work was finished.

'Never again,' said Charteris, looking with pride at the piles of *Glow Worms* stacked on the table; 'this jelly business makes one beastly sticky. I think we'll keep to print in future.'

And they did. Out of the twenty or more numbers of *The Glow Worm* published during Charteris' stay at School, that was the only one that did not come from the press. Readers who have themselves tried jellygraphing will sympathize. It is a curious operation, but most people will find one trial quite sufficient. That special number, however, reached a record circulation. The School had got its journey-money by the time it appeared, and wanted something to read in the train. Jim's pound was raised with ease.

Charteris took it round to him at the Babe's house, together with a copy of the special number.

'By Jove,' said Jim. 'Thanks awfully. Do you know, I'd absolutely forgotten all about *The Glow Worm*. I was to have written something for this number, wasn't I?'

And, considering the circumstances, that remark, as Charteris was at some pains to explain to him at the time, contained – when you came to analyse it – more cynical immorality to the cubic foot than any other half-dozen remarks he (Charteris) had ever heard in his life.

'It passes out of the realm of the merely impudent,' he said, with a happy recollection of a certain favourite author of his, 'and soars into the boundless empyrean of pure cheek.'

THE END

TITLES IN THE EVERYMAN WODEHOUSE

The Adventures of Sally
Aunts Aren't Gentlemen
Bachelors Anonymous
Barmy in Wonderland
Big Money
Bill the Conqueror
Blandings Castle
Bring on the Girls
Carry On, Jeeves
The Clicking of Cuthbert
Cocktail Time
The Code of the Woosters
The Coming of Bill
Company for Henry
A Damsel in Distress
Do Butlers Burgle Banks?
Doctor Sally
Eggs, Beans and Crumpets
A Few Quick Ones
French Leave
Frozen Assets
Full Moon
Galahad at Blandings
A Gentleman of Leisure
The Girl in Blue
The Girl on the Boat
The Gold Bat
The Head of Kay's
The Heart of a Goof
Heavy Weather
Hot Water
Ice in the Bedroom
If I Were You
Indiscretions of Archie
The Inimitable Jeeves
Jeeves and the Feudal Spirit
Jeeves in the Offing
Jill the Reckless
Joy in the Morning
Kid Brady Stories
Laughing Gas
Leave it to Psmith
The Little Nugget
Lord Emsworth and Others
Louder and Funnier
Love Among the Chickens
The Luck of the Bodkins
The Luck Stone
A Man of Means
The Man Upstairs
The Man with Two Left Feet
The Mating Season
Meet Mr Mulliner
Mike and Psmith
Mike at Wrykyn
The Military Invasion of America
Money for Nothing
Money in the Bank
Mr Mulliner Speaking
Much Obliged, Jeeves
Mulliner Nights
My Man Jeeves
Not George Washington
Nothing Serious
The Old Reliable
Over Seventy

Pearls, Girls and Monty Bodkin
A Pelican at Blandings
Performing Flea
Piccadilly Jim
Pigs Have Wings
Plum Pie
The Pothunters
A Prefect's Uncle
The Prince and Betty
Psmith in the City
Psmith, Journalist
Quick Service
Right Ho, Jeeves
Ring for Jeeves
Sam the Sudden
Service with a Smile
The Small Bachelor
Something Fishy
Something Fresh
Spring Fever
Stiff Upper Lip, Jeeves
Summer Lightning
Summer Moonshine
Sunset at Blandings
The Swoop!
Tales of St Austin's
Tales of Wrykyn and Elsewhere
Thank You, Jeeves
Ukridge
Uncle Dynamite
Uncle Fred in the Springtime
Uneasy Money
Very Good, Jeeves!
The White Feather
Young Men in Spats

This edition of P. G. Wodehouse has been prepared from the first British printing of each title.

The Everyman Wodehouse is printed on acid-free paper and set in Caslon, a typeface designed and engraved by William Caslon of William Caslon & Son, Letter-Founders in London around 1740.